Uncle

and the
Truth about magic

Jeremy Hullah

Digit Publications

First published in Great Britain in 2024 by Digit Publications
www.digitpublications.com

ISBN 978-1-7393579-3-1

Text copyright © Jeremy Hullah 2024
Illustrations copyright © Zsuzsa Goodyer 2024

The moral rights of the author and illustrator have been asserted.

This novel is a work of fiction. Names, characters, places, events and incidents are either the products of the author's imagination or used in a fictitious manner. Any resemblance to actual persons, living or dead, or actual events is purely coincidental.

All rights reserved in all media.

No part of this publication may be reproduced, stored in retrieval system, copied in any form or by any means, electronic, mechanical, photocopying, recording or otherwise transmitted without written permission from the author and/or publisher. You must not circulate this book in any format. Any person who does any unauthorised act in relation to this publication may be liable to criminal prosecution and civil claims for damages.

A CIP catalogue record for this book is available from the British Library.

Typesetting by the author

Printed and bound by CPI Group (UK) Ltd, Croydon CR0 4YY

Produced in United Kingdom

For Tom and Hugh

Always my first audience

Contents

Part 4: Alfred

Part 5: Endings and Legends

Epilogue

Prologue

A man sat in a wheelchair.

He was not so old that you would think, "he's old," and not so young that you would think, "he's young." His eyes still had the intensity of youth, but his hands were beginning to hold the lines that marked someone as having moved beyond middle age.

He was staring at a computer screen sitting on the desk in front of him.

It was blank.

The experience of his many successful years of writing had never made this moment easy: the beginning of a new book.

But this one was different.

He picked up the mug to the right of his keyboard and took a sip of hot tea. To the left of the keyboard was a pile of notebooks – all neatly in order, all containing the handwritten ideas and jottings of his much younger self, telling a story he had not yet told.

The story of how it all began.

He had tried many times to tell this first story, but it was too personal, too close to his pain, containing a heady mixture of fact and fiction that blurred the lines between his real life and his fantasy world.

But now the time had come.

He opened the first notebook and turned the pages, remembering.

This is how it started.

He listened to the sounds of years gone by, ringing dimly in his memories, and began to write.

Part 1: Sunshine and Clouds
Chapter 1
Clouds

This is a story about stories and the magic of stories.

This is a story of singing bears who speak in dreams and of beings made of light and darkness whose battle for power could destroy the world.

Although I become a part of this story, it's not my story; it's the story of my uncle – Uncle Digit.

The story happened more than forty years ago when I was a boy, in a time when there was no internet or social media, and if anyone mentioned 'climate' and 'change' in the same sentence, they were probably talking about the leaves turning red in autumn.

Even after all this time, I can close my eyes and smell the sharp tang of fresh oranges being squeezed for cakes. I can hear the clatter of bowls and pans in the kitchen as my mum cooked, and I can feel the youthful excitement of an eleven-year-old boy, as he sat in his wheelchair, listening to his uncle telling him incredible tales from around the world.

Our home was a large, terraced house full of our family history. My grandparents had moved there after they were married, just before the Second World War, and there were photos of them on sideboards and mantelpieces throughout the house: Alfred and Lily on their wedding day; Alfred in his Petty Officer's uniform before being shipped out to war; Alfred and Lily holding a very tiny Uncle Henry; Alfred with a kit bag on his shoulder as he left for an expedition a few years after the war – an expedition from which he would never return.

When Lily died suddenly at the age of fifty-five, Mum and Dad came to live in the house and I was born a few years later – Finnegan Starling Wake, or Finn for short. My father was Richard Wake and the Starling came from my mother, Tibby Starling. Mum said that Finnegan was only meant to be a 'working title' while she was pregnant, as it was a joke about some famous book. In the end though, they decided they liked Finn better than any other name and I was stuck with it.

A lot of the furniture, books, ornaments and vases in the house were remnants from Alfred and Lily and they had their own stories that Mum would tell me over and over. There were books that Mum read to me that her mother had read to her as a child. An old oak settle in the hallway that had belonged to Lily's father used to be Mum's favourite hiding place when she was a girl and some of the vases had little labels on the bottom, with tiny writing, showing where and when Alfred and Lily had bought them.

Mum and Dad's stuff nestled inbetween the older furniture and artefacts in a cosy jumble of styles that hadn't changed for as long as I could remember. Photos of Mum and

Dad's wedding, holidays and me, sat alongside photos of Lily and Alfred or Uncle Henry.

There was a good-sized sitting room downstairs, but that was only used to watch telly as we spent most of our time in the kitchen.

The kitchen took up half of the ground floor with a large range, hanging rails for pots, pans and ladles, and shelves full of jars of dried ingredients and spices. There was a huge dresser, jammed full of glasses and crockery, and a table in the middle of the room big enough to seat ten people.

Mum spent a great deal of time in the kitchen and it is there that my fondest memories lie; among the smells of the herbs and spices simmering in saucepans, and the light shining through the flour in the air as Mum baked bread, pies and sweet puddings.

She was always calmer when she was cooking. It was in the kitchen, more than anywhere else, that I heard her laughter, like the sound of glass bells, brightening up the room.

It was cooking that allowed her time to relax, and to forget that my dad had been taken from us and I'd been left paralysed by a car accident when I was four. To forget that we had very little money, because she was only able to work part-time and occasionally had to take in lodgers to make up the shortfall.

The lodgers stayed infrequently, but when they were there, they cast a shadow over the whole house I couldn't escape from, even in the kitchen or my own bedroom.

Most of them were pretty decent, but some weren't very nice at all. I remember one running out of the house, clutching his bag and a bloodied nose, screaming something about fetching the police and that Mum should think herself lucky someone was prepared to even look at her, considering.

"Considering what?" I asked Mum, confused. But she just gave me a big hug and sobbed into my shoulder. Those were the worst times. I would try my best to cheer Mum up by writing little stories about each lodger after they'd left. There was Awkward Andy, who broke things, and Skinny Simon, whose knees creaked and cracked as he walked. Then there was Huge Harry, who loved his little sports car more than anything in the world. But the car was too small for him and I wrote about him trying to fit in it with everything popping out and flying everywhere. That made mum laugh for a week.

The other thing that cheered her up was her brother coming to visit. I could always tell when he'd arrived, as Mum let out a little squeal of delight when she opened the door.

He would burst into the kitchen to say hello and I would almost jump out of my wheelchair with excitement. It was like the sun coming out after a month of rain. You forgot what it was like to be wet and miserable, and just enjoyed the bright sunshine and warmth.

My uncle talked endlessly about his adventures, making grand gestures with his arms as I sat motionless in awed silence.

Mum would laugh, saying, "Oh, for goodness' sake,

Henry! You'll have Finn believing you've actually done all those things."

He'd always smile broadly and wink after telling his stories, and this confused me – I didn't know if it meant he was making them up or not. He would look at my puzzled face and laugh as if it were the best joke in the world. But once or twice he would tap his nose when Mum had left the room and whisper to me, "You know that the wink's just for your mother, don't you, Dear Boy? It's all true, every word of it, but I wouldn't want her to get upset thinking I was actually running around doing mad things all the time, eh! So, just between you and me, okay?"

If he wasn't telling me his real-life adventures, we would be making up stories and sketches of our own. Like the spitfire pilots, meeting up after the war in reduced circumstances, always trying to show each other that everything was still 'tickety-boo': "I haven't *sold* the Jag dear boy, I've just lent it out to some film types who needed it for a shoot." And I was as likely to be called 'Dear Boy', 'Champ', or 'Sport' after the characters in these stories as by my own name.

Every time he came, he would bring something for me from his travels; sand from inside the great pyramids that no one had walked on for five thousand years, or bits of fossilised trees from the lost forests of Namibia, now nothing but dried-up waterfalls and deserts. He told me he tried to bring me something far more precious; that on the coast there were dunes where the diamonds lay on the surface of the sand and you could see them clearly at night as they glistened in the moonlight, but they were heavily guarded and he was chased away before he could get one.

Once, he brought me a squashed-up bullet that had missed him by two inches when he was covering a war in Lebanon, which he told me I must never show to Mum. Each present was the starting point for one of his fantastic stories, which I would listen to with eager ears and wide-open eyes.

When he left, I would be sad for days. Mum would have to work extra hard to cheer me up, even though I'm sure she'd have loved him to stay for longer as well.

"Can't you come and live with us?" I asked him. "You always give Mum some money when you leave, so why don't you just stay here all the time and look after us properly?"

"I couldn't do that, Finn. I'm just not reliable enough," he said. "I'm never around. There's nothing I'd love to do more, though. You know that, don't you? But I need to earn a living as well."

He was a photojournalist. At the time I didn't really know what that meant, or how a photojournalist made a living. I knew he did, of course, because of the extra money he gave Mum. Once, this was quite a lot and Mum stood there looking at the roll of notes in her hand.

"Henry, this is far too much," she protested. "What are you going to live on?"

He folded her hand gently over the money, saying something about selling a lot of pictures.

Sometimes he would look like he hadn't eaten or changed his clothes for a week, but he would always have something for Mum.

Then came the day it all started.

I'd just had an argument with Mum and she'd stormed off to answer the front door, leaving me in a mood that lifted only slightly when my uncle put his head around the kitchen door a few minutes later.

His beaming smile faltered when he saw me struggling to raise one of my own.

"What's up, Champ?" he asked, putting a magazine down on the kitchen table.

"It's nothing," I said, knowing he wouldn't believe me.

To avoid meeting his eyes, I looked at the cover of the magazine he'd put down. It was a photograph of a young girl standing in front of some ruined buildings.

"Did you take this?" I asked.

"Yes, I did."

"It looks so unreal; like it's another world."

"In a way, it is another world, but it's very real, I can assure you."

"Why do you have to go so far away?" I asked, with more frustration than I meant to. "Why can't you just take photographs around here?"

"I wish I could," he said, kneeling down in front of me. "But it's not as easy as that."

"Why not? If you were here, Mum wouldn't have to take people in," I blurted out, sinking down into my chair, as if this would make me invisible.

It didn't matter that there weren't any lodgers at that time; word got around school and there were always the occasional taunts, especially from Percy Simmons and Jasper Anderson in the year above. They called me 'Spinny' and delighted in seeing how long it would take before I started shouting at them, knowing that I couldn't get out of my chair to give them the thumping they deserved. But that day I didn't say anything.

"How much do you think Spinny's Mum charges the lodgers, Percy?" Anderson asked Simmons casually as they walked past me in the playground.

"Well," said Simmons with a pretend look of shock on his face. "I'm sure I can't guess. My mum says it depends what additional services she offers." And they both creased up laughing.

I had no idea what they found so funny, but I knew it wouldn't be anything pleasant.

"Or maybe," continued Simmons, as though thinking hard about something. "She just needs the company." He jutted his bottom lip out in mock sadness and pretended to cry. "She's been so very, very wonelee since she lost her husband." And they fell about again.

Before I knew it, I was charging towards them as fast as my hands could turn the wheels of my chair. Simmons and Anderson were too busy laughing to notice and I got right between them and knocked them over onto the hard tarmac surface.

Simmons was the brains of the pair who never got his hands dirty. He was looking shocked and was backing away on his bottom with one of his hands, the other feeling the blood oozing from a graze on his head. Anderson was the henchman and would think nothing of stamping on someone's foot to force them to give him their Mars Bar. He picked himself up straight away and launched himself at me, toppling me over and getting caught up in the wheels in the process, before the playground teacher came and separated us.

Mum was called in for a 'chat' after school. When we got home she let me know exactly what would happen if she was ever called in again.

Uncle Henry was looking at me, but I was staying stubbornly silent.

"Your mother tells me you got into trouble at school today?" he said, eventually.

I was shocked. Why had Mum told him? That made everything so much worse. I imagined sinking even lower into my chair, falling through the house and through the earth, into some lost world of caverns where nobody could find me. But it was no use; I could still hear my uncle talking. "Don't you want to tell me what happened?" he said.

No, I didn't.

"Didn't Mum tell you?" I said, my head firmly lowered onto my chest.

"Yes, she did, but I want to hear it from you."

"Why? It's not going to change anything, is it?" I shouted, right into his face, unable to stop myself. "They deserved it. They were saying horrible things about Mum and the lodgers!"

He pulled up a chair and sat down, letting me calm myself for a minute until I felt bad for shouting at him.

"I'm sorry, I didn't mean to shout at you. Sometimes I just want things to be different and I'm angry when they're not. Is that wrong?"

"It's not wrong to want to change things, Finn. It can be a good thing that helps you develop and become a better person. But it's also important to know what you can change."

I didn't say anything for a while, allowing his words to sink in and calm me further. I found myself staring at the photo of the girl on the magazine cover. Her dark hair was matted and covered in dust, her clothes were frayed and torn, and she was holding a doll tightly to her chest. The most striking thing about her were her searing blue eyes, which were looking straight into the camera, challenging you to an impossible staring competition.

"Who's the girl?" I asked.

"She's a princess," replied my uncle.

"She doesn't look like a princess."

"Really?" he said, looking at the picture as if for the first time. "Yes, I see what you mean. But look closer and you'll see the camera shows more than just dirt and torn clothes. What else can you see?"

I looked again, but I could only see the buildings and the girl.

"What was the first thing you noticed when you looked at it?" he asked.

"I think it was her eyes," I said.

"When you look at her eyes, what do you see?"

"She looks angry."

"Yes, and anything else? Does she look afraid?"

"Not really; she looks defiant, as if something's burning inside her, like fire."

Uncle Digit smiled. "I couldn't have put it better myself, Dear Boy. I got to know this girl a little and I got to know her fire a bit more. It was her courage, her strength and her heart that made her a princess."

I was still looking at the photo, wondering at a life so different from my own.

"She reminds me of a fairy tale your grandmother used to tell me and your mother when we were young," my uncle continued. "She called it 'The Truth About Magic'. I'd ask her to tell it to me whenever I felt a bit like I think you do now. Has your mother ever told it to you?"

"Not that I remember, no." I wasn't sure how a fairy tale was going to help me.

"Do you want to hear it?"

I shook myself out of my doldrums, reminding myself that even though this wasn't going to be one of his amazing stories from his travels, just listening to my uncle talk made me feel better.

"Yes, please," I said.

And my uncle told me the following story.

Chapter 2

The Truth about Magic

Once upon a time, there was a princess who lived in a castle with her parents, the king and queen.

The princess had always been outgoing and refused to be tied down to life in the castle. Her parents were forever sending out the guards to fetch her back from playing with the children in the town, or from wandering around the markets.

But she was bright and had a mind as quick and sharp as a guillotine. She never neglected her studies and if she wasn't running around outside the castle, she would be spending time with her tutor, who was also the king's sorcerer.

As the king's sorcerer, her tutor performed valuable services for the kingdom, such as blessing the wells with sweet water or charming the land so that it produced bountiful crops.

The tutor admired the princess greatly for her intelligence and thoughtfulness. She didn't just ask questions about everything; she thought deeply about the answers and asked a more searching question afterwards.

This was how she'd found out the conjurings her tutor performed to entertain the court were merely tricks and that there was nothing special in the other tasks he carried out.

"You mean there's no such thing as magic?" the princess had asked when she discovered this.

"If people want to believe in magic," her tutor replied, "That is what they will see."

One day, a wandering sorcerer passed through the kingdom and visited the castle. He amazed the king and queen with demonstrations of magic, in which he hurled fireballs over the town walls and turned small amounts of dust into gold.

The sorcerer offered his services to the king and queen, claiming that he desired nothing more than a living in return.

The king and queen thought of everything that could be achieved with the help of such great magic. They could make their kingdom safe from invasion and their people would want for nothing.

The tutor and the princess were frightened by this talk, though.

"But these are just tricks," the princess said, stamping her feet.

"Yes, but why is he doing it, do you think?" asked her tutor. "These tricks can't really do what your father and mother hope for. The sorcerer must have some other motive for offering his services."

They waited until they were alone with the king and queen.

"Your majesties," the tutor began. "You have always listened to my counsel, so I hope you will listen to me now when I tell you this sorcerer can't be trusted. What he has shown you is not magic. They are just tricks to impress you for some reason. And I'm afraid of what that reason might be."

16

"You are indeed my trusted counsellor," replied the king. "But I also have to trust my own eyes. We all saw the fireballs bursting outside the walls of the town, and I have the gold that the sorcerer made here in my pocket. Maybe you're jealous that your magic can't achieve these things."

"I can't do these things, sire, because they are not possible."

"But we've seen your magic do impossible things," countered the king. "We've seen you turn our daughter's flower drawings into real blooms."

The tutor sighed. He showed the king and queen that the 'magic' he had performed to turn the princess's drawings into real flowers was just a trick. He begged them to see that the sorcerer's magic also wasn't real; that is was just tricks of light and movement.

Instead of believing him, the king and queen were so shocked to learn he'd deceived them that they banished him from the castle for being a false sorcerer.

The princess pleaded with her parents to believe her tutor, but they were adamant. And when she showed them that even she could perform some of her tutor's tricks, her parents were so angry they banished her from the castle as well, telling her she could only return when she could show she understood the foolishness of what she'd done.

So, with heavy hearts and great sadness, the princess and her tutor left the castle and went to live in the town among the people.

Shortly afterwards, the king and queen fell sick. The sorcerer announced they were being attacked by dark forces wanting to invade their kingdom. Extra taxes were imposed to pay for everything necessary to battle this new enemy and to save the town and the king and queen.

For many weeks, the townspeople saw flashes of light and heard terrifying howling coming from the castle tower where the sorcerer was doing battle with the evil power that was trying to destroy the king and the queen.

But life under the new sorcerer was going badly for the people, who could ill afford the extra taxes they now had to pay. A number of them marched to the castle.

"We're hungry!" they cried.

"You've put a spell on our king and queen!" someone shouted out.

"You're making yourself rich on our taxes!" shouted others.

"I bet that's just a lot of light and noise coming from the castle," someone else said.

Others agreed and they started shouting out "Fraud!", "Trickster!", and "Go home!"

The sorcerer suddenly appeared on the castle balcony. Without saying anything, he raised his arms and flames burst from his hands. The crowd turned and screamed in despair as fireballs exploded in the town, destroying buildings and killing and injuring many people.

Everyone became afraid and no one spoke against the sorcerer anymore.

The princess and her tutor weren't afraid, though, and when a grand parade was announced to celebrate the one-year anniversary of the sorcerer keeping everyone safe from the dark forces, they made a plan that they hoped would free the whole town.

When the day of the parade arrived, the princess made sure she was in the middle of the market square with the other townsfolk.

The sorcerer rode in a splendid open carriage. He was dressed in glittering robes and held a jewelled cane, which he waved at the silent crowds. He was unmoved by the silence and smiled at everyone, seemingly enjoying the fear in the people's eyes.

As his carriage moved past the princess, she stepped forward and smiled up at him, holding out a basket of flowers.

The sorcerer looked down, surprised to see the princess standing there, and tapped the driver with his cane to stop the carriage next to her.

"I want to thank you for everything you have done for the town and for my parents," she said, speaking clearly.

The sorcerer smiled at her and bowed his head, acknowledging her thanks. But as he leant forward to take the basket from her, the princess pulled some rotten vegetables from under the flowers and threw them at the sorcerer, smearing the rich brocade of his robe with their putrid juices.

He cried out in anger and the townsfolk gasped. Some of them ran away in fear of what the sorcerer would do next.

The sorcerer stared at the princess with a cruel smile on his face.

"Which building would you like to see burnt to the ground first?" he sneered.

The sorcerer knew very well that she wouldn't be able to answer this and waited for her to apologise to him for the insult.

But the princess said nothing. Reaching inside her basket again, she took out a rotten egg and threw it at the sorcerer, striking him on the head and leaving foul-smelling slime trailing down his face.

"The whole town will suffer for what you've done!" the sorcerer screamed in rage.

He raised his hands to send out fireballs and everyone cowered, expecting the worst. But although flames burst from his hands as before, no fireballs erupted anywhere in the town. Nothing happened.

The sorcerer stared wildly around the square, looking for something, his face contorted with anger and confusion.

The princess smiled, fully aware of what the sorcerer was searching for.

She and her tutor knew the sorcerer must have had accomplices to create the explosions that made everyone believe he was magically casting fireballs. By carefully watching, listening and talking to people, the princess and her tutor had discovered who these accomplices were, and by using some 'magic' of his own, the tutor had made sure these people were all asleep and tied up.

"Where's your magic now?" the princess asked the sorcerer, smiling.

He looked down at the princess with a mixture of rage and bewilderment. With a strangled cry he looked back into the town and raised his hands again to release fireballs. But still nothing happened and the sorcerer turned desperately to the soldiers. "Arrest the princess!" he bellowed at them, his face contorted with fury.

But the guards didn't move.

Then the sorcerer felt something hit his back and he swung around to stare at the princess again. But the princess hadn't thrown anything.

The townsfolk were picking themselves up and moving slowly towards the sorcerer. As they walked forwards, they gathered up anything they could find from the ground and hurled it at him, pelting straw, dirt and rubbish at him until he was covered from head to foot in filth and grime.

The first people to reach the carriage dragged the sorcerer out and handed him to the soldiers to lock up.

The princess and the tutor went straight to the castle. It wasn't long before they found the poisons used by the sorcerer to keep the king and queen ill all the time.

They carefully nursed the king and queen back to health. The princess didn't leave their sides until they had recovered well enough to walk around and show themselves to the people who gathered daily outside the castle, waiting for news.

From that day, no one believed in magic anymore. The princess and the tutor still entertained everyone by performing tricks, but everyone knew they were just tricks. The princess even showed them how the tricks were done after she'd performed them.

Chapter 3

Sunshine

"And they all lived happily ever after?" I asked, smiling.

"Yes, they all lived happily ever after," said my uncle, smiling back. "What did you think of it?"

"It's a bit strange having a fairy story with no magic in it. It's kind of the wrong way around, isn't it?"

"I think that's the point," said my uncle. "It's like looking at the world through the wrong end of a telescope. When someone turns it round for you, everything becomes that much more real. It was the people in the story who were living in a fairy tale, wasn't it? The princess was the defiant one; she got them to turn the telescope round the right way. That's the real magic."

I thought about this. "So, am I looking at things the wrong way round?"

"No, it's not that," he said. "Your grandmother varied the story with each telling, but every time she finished, she asked us if we were like the king and the queen, wanting something magical to change things we couldn't control, or if we were like the princess, having the courage to question and change those things we could."

"And you always chose the princess?" I said.

"Yes," said Uncle Henry. "But more importantly, it made

me think about the things I wanted to change and the things I couldn't."

"You mean like not having a dad?" I said quietly.

Like me, my uncle had also lost his father when he was young. It was one of the things that drew us closer together. The ship on which Alfred left to go on his expedition had disappeared somewhere in the Arctic, shortly after the Second World War, when Uncle Henry was five. There had been one or two attempts to locate the ship, but no one had ever found it.

"That's something you definitely can't change, yes," he said. "But it could be something more mundane, like your mother having to take in lodgers."

"Oh," I said. "Back to that again."

"That's where this all started, remember?" he said. "The lodgers aren't something you or I can control. I can help out with some money occasionally, but taking in paying guests is something your mother controls, to make sure you and she have everything you need."

"So, it's not something I should be fighting against?"

"No. There's no magic wand here; it's something you have to learn to accept. If people say mean things, there are better ways to deal with it than running them over!"

I was quiet until he leant forward to tousle my hair.

"Come on, Sport," he said. "Don't you want to know where I'm off to next?"

And there was the sun again. "Of course," I said.

"It actually concerns your grandfather," he said. "You remember me telling you about the dreams I have?"

He'd often told me about the dreams he had of his father's ship. He said they were so real it was like watching a film. He even described the snow-covered mountains on the coast near where the ship was supposed to have disappeared, as though he had seen them with his own eyes. Mum said he was obsessed and had an over-active imagination, but my uncle always maintained that he'd find the ship one day.

"You're going to look for the ship?" I said.

"Yes, I am. Can you believe it?"

"But didn't Granddad disappear in the Arctic Circle?"

"Yes."

"How are you going to get there?" I said. "I thought only scientific expeditions went that far."

"Well, that's the interesting bit…" He paused dramatically, settling in for another story. "There's an expedition going up there soon and they commissioned me to photograph their work for a journal."

"What are they doing?"

"They're measuring the glaciers and the permafrost – the frozen ground," he explained, seeing my puzzled look.

"How do you measure a glacier?" I asked.

"That, I'm not sure," he said. "The expedition is trying to establish whether the glaciers and permafrost are melting. If they're right, it will prove the Earth is getting warmer. In a decade or so, by the turn of the century, the world will be half a degree hotter."

"That doesn't sound much," I said.

"It doesn't, does it," he conceded. "By itself it could probably be ignored. But if the trend continues, by 2020 this increase will be one and half degrees and by 2040 it could be as high as four degrees."

"Is that bad?"

"Yes, it is."

"Oh."

"You might not remember, but the ship your grandfather was on was doing the same thing."

"Measuring glaciers?" I asked. This was news to me.

"Something like that," he said. "After the war, some people noticed the temperature in the Tropics was changing. They wanted to see if it was limited to that region or if it was a global phenomenon. So they organised an expedition to the Arctic."

"To the same place?"

"More or less. My father never got to where they were meant to be going, but this expedition will be based only a hundred miles or so from where his ship went missing."

"Can you show me on a map?" Some of my uncle's excitement was rubbing off on me. "I've got a big atlas on the shelf in my room."

He got up and went upstairs to get the atlas, coming down

a minute later and opening it up on the kitchen table at some pages that were all white and covered in mountains.

"It's a bit small and hard to see, but the base is about here," he said, pointing at the map. Then he pointed to part of the sea not far from the coast to the northeast.

"The last radio message from your grandfather's ship came from the sea, just about here," he said. "The message said there was a storm approaching and they were heading for the shelter of this bay here." He pointed to a large circular bay almost completely surrounded by mountains.

"But aren't the mountains that you dream of sort of circular?"

"Yes," he said. "But that's not unusual. Lots of mountain ranges like this are formed from old volcanoes."

"But if the last radio message was at sea, how do you know the ship ended up in the bay?"

"I don't really," he said. "But that's where I would go if I wanted to get away from a big storm."

"When are you leaving?"

"Well, that's the sad part. I have to go on Sunday morning."

It was Friday.

"Oh!" All my excitement evaporated.

"I know," he said. "I'm sorry, Finn, but it's not for long. I'll be back before you know it with stories that'll make your hair stand on end."

"You'd better."

Spring was flowing into summer and it was starting to get warm. Uncle Henry took me on a long walk, pushing my wheelchair to places I couldn't take myself, down forest tracks to still places by water where dragonflies darted and the silence was broken only by the sound of birdsong and the soft buzz of insects.

We talked and talked. He told me stories from his travels and I asked him questions about the world. He seemed to know everything from how bees talked to each other, to how the universe worked.

In the evening, we chatted and played games with my mum. Then on Monday he left, taking part of the sun with him.

Part 2: Uncle Digit
Chapter 4

One Digit

The 'not for long' my uncle promised when he left turned out to be 'for a very long time'.

After a week, I got a postcard from him with a picture of snow-covered mountains.

> Dear Finn,
>
> This is the last piece of civilisation for thousands of miles.
> No phones. Will write when I can.
> Let the adventure begin!
>
> Uncle Henry

But after that, I heard nothing.

It was halfway through the summer term by now and I was in the playground with one of my best friends, Freddy Wells, who was a couple of years older than me. He was a bit awkward at times and had a slight stutter, but he was by far the smartest person I knew. We had bonded over our love of the stars and crazy stories and we would spend most break times chatting about absolutely anything that came into our heads that might start a new flow of ideas going.

That day though, we were just hanging around in the playground, wilting slightly under a June heatwave. Katie Barnes and her friend Alice walked over and sat on a small wall near us and we chatted about our various plans for the holidays.

Katie was pretty and sporty and everyone liked her, including me. Simmons and Anderson chose that moment to wander past and Simmons gave a little laugh as he caught sight of me talking to Katie and Alice.

"I'd be careful of that Starling Wake boy, Barnes," Simmons drawled at Katie. "He has a nasty habit of running people over if he doesn't like what they're saying."

"Well, there's no chance of that happening with Katie, is there?" I burst out angrily before I could stop myself, regretting that I had let Simmons get to me so easily.

Anderson gave an absurd theatrical laugh. "Are you actually trying to chat up Barnes, Spinny?" he snorted. "In what strange fantasy world would a girl like Katie Barnes ever be interested in someone like you?" He made it clear that he meant someone in a wheelchair.

"Shut up, Anderson." Katie said in shock, looking at me with concern to see what I would do.

My hands were itching on the rims of my chair wheels and I could feel myself going red with anger and embarrassment. I tried to calm myself by remembering what

Uncle Henry had told me. He said that there were better ways of dealing with people. But what? My mind was too full of anger to think straight.

Freddy suddenly looked up at the two boys.

"D-do you know…" he started to say.

"D-d-do I know wh-wh-what, Wo-Wo-Wells?" Anderson mocked, and he and Simmons started laughing,

A few more kids nearby stopped to watch what was taking place with a mixture of curiosity and distaste. Freddy showed no signs of being angered by Anderson and waited patiently for the two boys to stop laughing.

"I was g-going to say, Anderson," Freddy began, in an even, conversational manner. "That g-girls can be very c-complicated and q-quite hard to understand sometimes."

I wondered where Freddy was going with this and Simmons and Anderson had stopped still, equally interested to know what was coming next.

"I've known g-girls," Freddy continued. "Who refused to g-go out with boys with perfectly g-good bodies," and here, Freddy indicated Anderson as if for an example. "Simply because they were c-complete and utter j-jerks."

Katie and Alice both shrieked "Yes!" and doubled over laughing. A few of the other kids who were watching also laughed out loud. Anderson's face turned bright red, his eyes narrowing to thin slits, his lips curling back over his teeth.

"Why you…" he snarled, striding towards Freddy with

fists clenched.

Although Freddy might have been the brightest person I knew, he wouldn't last ten seconds against Anderson. I was getting ready to do some more ramming when Katie got up suddenly from the wall and put herself between Freddy and Anderson.

"What're you going to do, Anderson?" she asked contemptuously. "Prove him right?"

Anderson stopped and glared into Katie's face. "I'm going to teach him a lesson."

"Well," she said. "You'll have to go through me first. And won't that make you the big boy!" She poked a finger in his chest.

Simmons pulled on Anderson's sleeve. "Just leave it, Jasper," he urged, tugging harder to try and make Anderson move. Anderson moved his face closer to Katie's. "This isn't over, Barnes," he sneered, letting himself be dragged away.

That was the best day. We all went back to our separate classes with huge grins on our faces. I couldn't wait to tell Uncle Henry about it, but there was still no word from him.

Another month passed and I stopped being able to think about anything else. I started asking Mum if she'd heard anything so often that she posted a big note on the kitchen noticeboard. It said:

Uncle Henry Whereabouts: Not Known.

There was a date attached, so I'd know she hadn't heard

anything that day.

Then one evening, a week or so after the notice appeared, my mum came into the sitting room.

I was watching the latest episode of Only Fools and Horses. Granddad had just released the wrong chandelier from a ceiling, which crashed to the floor as Rodney and Del Boy watched in horror from beneath the other chandelier they'd been expecting to catch. I was laughing so much that I didn't see Mum holding out a letter for me.

"Finn," she said. "You might want to see this."

I looked up and took the letter from her as the credits rolled and Del Boy, Rodney and Granddad made their hasty exit.

"It's from Uncle Henry!" I said excitedly.

"Who did you expect?" she said, sitting on the sofa next to me. "Not many other people write to you, do they?"

I weighed the letter in my hands, savouring the moment, drawing out the seconds until I would open it.

"It's quite fat," I said, looking at the unfamiliar stamp with the postmark from somewhere I'd never heard of. Turning the envelope over, I saw a couple of blue crayon lines with indecipherable writing scrawled between them. I wondered how many other hands had touched the letter before it came to rest in mine.

"Aren't you going to open it?" asked Mum a little impatiently.

I prised the envelope open with my finger and took out a sheaf of pages, doubled over. As I unfolded them, something dropped onto my lap. I picked it up and looked at a photograph of Uncle Henry sitting up in what was obviously a hospital bed. He was smiling and holding up his left hand, showing four bandaged fingers, one of which was clearly much shorter than it should be. Looking more closely, I could see his lips were split and his nose was red and lined.

I turned the photograph over. Scribbled diagonally across it he had written:

I've lost a digit, Dear Boy, or part of one at least.

I felt Mum stiffen as she caught sight of the image of her brother in hospital. I didn't say anything and handed the photograph to her so she could see for herself. She looked at it with a mixture of shock and concern. "Oh no," she said. "What's he been up to now?"

"Looking for Granddad's lost ship, I expect."

"I know he has, but he can't go around losing bits of himself in the process."

I laughed and Mum looked at me sternly, then started to laugh herself.

"I wasn't being funny," she said, trying to sound angry.

I stopped laughing. "I'm sure he explains everything in the letter," I said. "Do you want me to read it to you?"

She sighed. "I suppose so."

I held the letter up and began to read:

"Dear Finn, as you can see, I've managed to get myself into a bit of a state. Don't worry, though, it's nothing serious and I'll be out of here in no time…"

"Nothing serious?!" Mum scoffed.

I carried on:

"… I'll be out of here in no time, then I'm going back to look for your granddad's ship, as the adventure has only just begun."

Mum groaned.

"I'll tell you what it's like here, so you get an idea of what we go through, living and working in these extreme conditions.

"You have to be on your guard every second when you travel on snow and ice. Even when the weather's fine, there are ice bridges that can collapse if you cross them at the wrong time of day, and crevasses that will take you hundreds or thousands of feet under the glaciers if you fall down them.

"Even though it's really cold, it sometimes rains. The wind whips up the rain and it lashes it into you like pellets. And there's always the cold, which never goes away until you're safely back in the station. Little icicles form from your nostrils and your eyebrows, and at times it gets so cold your nose can break off if you rub it too hard."

I looked at Mum in alarm.

"He's just exaggerating," she said. "You can't break your nose off."

I relaxed and returned to the letter:

"It's definitely the most hostile place I've ever been in, which is saying something considering there's no one trying to shoot you!"

"I suppose he thinks that's funny as well?!" Mum said with more than a hint of irritation.

"Do you want me to carry on?"

"Sorry."

"… I arranged with the team to hire what I needed to travel on my own for a week or so. I didn't need ropes in the mountains I was heading for, but I did need crampons for walking on ice. So I had those, along with camping equipment, rations for ten days, torches and a small flare gun that could be seen from twenty-five miles away in good weather if I got into trouble. It could also be used to scare anything that got too close. Then, I had a skidoo…" I stopped. "What's a skidoo?" I asked.

"It's a sort of motorbike on skis."

"They sound like a lot of fun."

"I'm sure they can be," said Mum. "But your uncle had a motorbike when he was younger and the thought of him flying across the snow on one of those things makes me very nervous."

"Well, let's see what he gets up to."

I read on.

"… I had a skidoo, a map, a good compass and the exact bearings that would take me to all the routes I needed over the mountains and back again.

"I had everything I needed. What could possibly go wrong?

"As it turned out, quite a bit.

"Once I was sure the weather would be good for a few days, I left.

"I took the skidoo as far as I could and left it in a sheltered place at the bottom of the first range of mountains I had to cross. I climbed the rest of the day, making camp out of the wind close to the summit. I ate supper, then lay there staring up at the stars. With no other light around, they come out in their billions, with the Milky Way stretched across the sky like a long line of candy floss. There was the universe. And here was I; one man on a mountain. An invisible dot on an invisible dot, as someone once said. I felt the whole night sky wrapping itself around me, making me part of this immense beauty. I crawled into my tent and slept like a log.

"I set off first thing in the morning, getting to the top of the mountain shortly afterwards. I looked across the long valley of white snow to the great circle of mountains on the other side, which was my final destination.

"From my higher vantage point, I saw the enormous circle of rock curving round, with an opening to the sea on the right-hand side. The tall, ragged, saw-toothed peaks jutted upwards, forbidding and inhospitable. Even the snow that concealed most of their surfaces couldn't hide the fact there was very little of it that could be crossed safely.

"I swept my gaze along the range and found what the maps of this region had shown. Looking as though a giant thumb had broken a piece off the top, there was a gap in the peaks where the lava flow had carved out a smooth valley as it poured down the side of the mountain, millions of years ago. That was my route into the bay.

"It took me a whole day to get down the mountain and walk across the snow-covered ground between the two ranges, stopping in the foothills to make camp.

"Then things started to get a little strange.

"I put up the tent and got things ready for the evening. The light was beginning to fade when something caught my eye. A light in the sky was heading towards me. It was like a star falling out of the heavens, but it shone and glistened like no star I'd ever seen before. All the colours of the rainbow flashed from it as it hurtled across the sky, passing right overhead without making a sound and continuing over the mountain and into the bay beyond. I waited to hear the sound of it hitting the ground, but there was nothing; just the gentle wind and the quiet of the evening.

"Then the sky behind the mountains started to glow with an eerie, pulsating light. I wondered if it could be the Northern Lights, but the light began to be split with flashes; bright streaks of blue and red bursting up into the darkening sky above.

"I watched dumbstruck, as this incomprehensible spectacle continued, knowing I wouldn't be able to find an explanation until tomorrow.

"Slowly the lights began to fade, until there were only the stars left to brighten the evening. I felt anxious about what I might find the next day and calmed myself by completing the routines required to continue setting the camp and cook my meal.

"I was just taking my first mouthful of food when I heard something and froze with the spoon halfway to my mouth.

"A deep roaring sound was disturbing the calm of the night, getting closer and louder, as if some immense animal in pain was rushing towards me. I stood up, still holding onto my food, listening to it get closer and closer.

Then there was no doubt: it was the monstrous howl of a storm. Even in the dim starlit night I could clearly see a wall of snow heading directly for me. I stood there, unable to move, wondering where it had come from.

"Then, it was too late.

"The tent was ripped from its fastenings and disappeared into the night, along with everything I'd taken from the backpack, including my sleeping bag. I just managed to grab the backpack before I was pushed to the ground by the force of the storm and rolled along like a bowling ball.

"I could see nothing as the snow swirled around me in a blur, and all I could hear was the deafening wind, like an aeroplane taking off next to me. I really thought that was it, that I was going to end up being smashed against something.

But it was my backpack that eventually slammed into an outcrop of rock, providing me with a bit of a cushion.

"I managed to crawl around the rock and sat there sheltered from the wind, hugging my backpack and waiting for the storm to blow itself out.

"Then, just as quickly as it had started, the storm ended. The roaring died to a whisper and the snow stopped swirling around and settled back down. I looked up and saw a sky full of stars without a single cloud in the sky.

"I was past wondering how the storm had suddenly appeared and disappeared. I knew I would need all my strength for the journey back, so I tried to get what sleep I could. I curled up and covered myself with anything I could find in the backpack that could give me some protection from the cold, including the backpack itself.

"It was impossible to do more than drift in and out of sleep, though, and I soon became so cold I could only lie there and shiver.

"As soon as it started to get light, I ate and drank as much as I could and headed off, feeling lost and defeated.

"I don't remember much about the journey back. I walked and climbed all day. I really don't know how I got down the mountain. I think I must have let myself slide or fall down a lot of it, judging by my bruises and cracked ribs.

"I knew I wouldn't survive if I spent another night outside, so I got myself to the skidoo somehow, pointed it in the right direction and let it take me from there.

"And that's about it. I got back to the station in one piece and they put me on the supply chopper to bring me here, to this hospital. The doctors did what they could for my frostbite, but they couldn't save my finger and had to remove part of it.

"I reckon I need another week here, then I'll head back.

"I'll be okay, though, and I don't want you or your mum to worry. I can't explain what happened in the mountains. I don't know what the meteor was and I don't know where the storm came from. They were freak events and they won't happen again. But, you never know – I might even find where the meteor landed.

"Whatever happens, I'll write and let you know everything.

"Your loving uncle, Henry."

I folded the letter and looked across at Mum. She was staring at the floor and I could see her mouth moving as she bit her bottom lip.

She looked up, eyes blazing. "I'm going to kill him!"

I gave a small laugh. "He seems to be doing a pretty good job of that himself."

"Finn!" she said, sounding shocked, as she got up and stormed out of the room.

Uncle Digit

Chapter 5

Two Digits

Uncle Henry wasn't mentioned in the house for a few days after that, though I never stopped thinking about him and imagining what he'd be doing or what he'd discover when he got across the mountains.

As the long summer holiday rolled on, I could see Mum getting more and more agitated as the days stretched out without any word from him.

Then, about a week after the start of the new school year, she came into my room with a parcel.

"Your uncle's sent you something," she said, unable to hide the excitement in her voice.

The parcel was the size of a shoe box. It was all brown paper and string with strange stamps and even more writing in blue crayon on both sides. Mum helped me with the string and I opened it with nervous hands full of eager anticipation.

Inside there was a letter addressed to Mum, a large wad of writing, tied up and addressed to me, some photographs, and a grey ball wrapped inside a lot of tissue paper.

I handed Mum her letter then picked up the photos. There were some of the mountains, including one from high up that showed the great circular mountain range he'd told me about before. There were also some of polar bears, with cubs playing around in the snow. And then there was one of him sitting up in a hospital bed, holding up his hands.

"Look, Mum, he's lost another finger."

I showed her the photograph. She put her letter down and her face crumpled up as if she was about to cry.

"Oh no, whenever is he going to stop this nonsense?" she said, handing it back to me.

I turned the photograph over. The words,

Look; I'm alright

were written across the back in big letters. I looked at the photo of him smiling and showing off his missing fingers. I could hear him saying, 'I've lost another digit, Dear Boy.'

"He calls them 'digits' you know," I told Mum.

"Does he?" said Mum. "Well, he can call them what he likes, but he can't go around losing any more of them."

I tried to imitate his slightly gruff and quick voice, "Dear Boy, I seem to have lost a couple of digits."

"Don't, it's not funny," said Mum, trying not to laugh.

I carried on in his voice. "In fact, I don't want you to call me Uncle Henry anymore, I want you to call me Uncle Digits. No, Uncle Digit sounds better, don't you think?"

Mum screwed her nose up. "I'm not sure either of them sound very nice."

I carried on in my own voice, "Well, it sort of suits him, doesn't it? Uncle Digit. I'm sure he would like it."

Mum didn't say anything else.

"What did he say to you in his letter?" I asked.

"Just that he's sorry to put us through this, but he's okay and we're not to worry. He says he's written you a story about what he got up to. Looks like it's more of a novel."

There were certainly a lot more pages than last time.

"And why's he sent you a ball, for goodness' sake?" she said.

"I don't know," I said, equally confused.

I looked at the ball, sitting in the box, half wrapped in tissue paper. It was about the size of a small grapefruit and looked completely smooth, with no marks of any kind. I reached down and stroked it, my fingers gliding so smoothly over the surface it was as though I wasn't touching anything. It was so smooth and perfect, it was impossible to tell if it was made of metal or plastic. What could it be?

I picked it up.

"What's up?" Mum asked.

The surprise must have been clear on my face.

"It's nothing," I said quickly. "Just that when I started to lift it, it felt really heavy, then it just came up in my hand."

I looked at the ball resting in my palm. Somehow it felt as though I was holding one of Uncle Digit's stories; as if all the wonderful strangeness and excitement I experienced when he spoke was all wrapped up inside this small, round object.

Mum looked at me with amusement. "I'm glad you like

it," she said. "Hopefully, when you've read his letter you'll be able to tell me why your uncle has sent you a grey ball from the ends of the Earth."

"I'm sure there'll be an explanation," I said.

"More likely it'll be part of some outlandish story that'll have you talking about nothing else for the next month."

She laughed her beautiful laugh and kissed me on the nose before getting up.

"I'm going to cook supper and leave you to read your letter in peace."

And so I read the letter, devouring every word, not knowing whether to believe anything I was reading or not, holding onto the ball all the time and wondering when I was going to find out what it was.

My Dearest Boy,

I hope the following pages will keep you amused until I return. They are my account of the most extraordinary adventure I've ever had.

Don't worry about showing it to your mother, as she won't believe any of it. But that's the way I want it. Only you will know that it's all true.

And it is.

Every word of it!

Chapter 6

Snow

Once I got back to the research station, I waited until I was confident that the weather would be calm for a few days, then set off again on the skidoo.

The journey back to the mountains was uneventful. After two days, I was at the bottom of the second mountain range. This time though, when I made camp, there were no strange lights and no storm to blow me off my feet. There was just me eating my supper, looking out at the stars, wondering what I was going to find the next day.

I woke up early, ate breakfast and started the ascent. It was much easier than the climb up the first mountain. This was just a long hard walk along the wide channel left by the lava flow.

It was just after midday when I found myself standing at the top, staring down at a scene from my dreams.

There was the same three-quarter circle of jagged mountains, sweeping around on either side of me, creating an opening to the sea in the east. The only detail that had been unclear in my dreams was the size of the bay: it must have been at least five miles across.

I tried to tell myself that there must be any number of craters in the world very similar to this, and that I was just willing it to look like something from my dreams.

But it had that strange familiar feel, like a photograph that I had studied for ages, which had become lodged in my memory.

After I got over my initial reaction, I started looking for signs of the meteor that had crashed here just a month before. I thought that even from up here I would have been able to see some evidence of where it had fallen – maybe a hole through the snow and sea-ice, or a mark on one of mountains, where something large and travelling at high speed had struck. But there was nothing. Not a single sign that anything had happened.

I saw the beautifully even snow field that covered the sea-ice within the curve of the mountain range. It looked like a perfectly smooth white disk that someone had carefully placed to cover the gigantic mouth of the volcano.

I wondered if any hole the meteor would have made through the snow and ice would have frozen over and filled up with snow again. I thought that even if it had, it should still have left some sort of mark, like the lines in fields you see from the air where old roads or ancient houses used to be.

I looked down at this vast, enclosed space and thought that if I could see no trace of a meteor that had landed here a few weeks ago, what chance had I of finding any trace of a ship after forty years had passed?

The hopelessness of my task suddenly dawned on me.

How did I think I would find anything? If the ship had sunk below the ice, there would be no trace of it and nothing to see. I started asking myself why I had been drawn here? What was I hoping to find? I couldn't really have believed that I would find the ship.

I sat eating my lunch, staring out at the view, so like my dreams. I wondered if maybe, just being here, looking at the spot where my father had last been alive on this Earth, was enough. That I should recognise that this was as far as I needed to go and that now I should go home and get on with my real life.

Packing up my stuff, I felt my mind clear. All thoughts about the ship, the meteor and everything else that I had wondered about were no longer spinning about screaming for answers.

I was completely calm, standing there, staring down at the bay. The almost perfect circle of rock and snow was incredibly beautiful. I thought that, as I had come this far, I could at least walk down the mountain and wander along the frozen shoreline for a time before heading back.

It took me until late afternoon to get down the mountain and I made camp near the bottom, close to the frozen sea.

I spent the rest of the day exploring the shoreline, like a child at the beach, turning over interesting coloured stones and seeing if there was anything living in the ice-cold rock pools.

I returned to my tent and ate, not really thinking about

anything.

I became fascinated by the snow lying on the surface of the frozen bay. I had never seen snow on sea-ice before, so didn't know if what I was seeing was normal or not. It was completely uniform and flat all the way to the other side, five miles in the distance. I could see no variation in the level; it was seemingly undisturbed by the wind above or the sea below.

I suddenly remembered one of my dreams; about a huge white circle of snow. Why was I remembering this now? There had been something about the other side. Something, or someone, had been on the other side. I stood up and tried to make out anything across the wide expanse, but I could see nothing in the dimming light.

I relaxed and told myself that it was just another coincidence.

I still had supplies and time. If I wanted to I could walk across the bay to the other side tomorrow, just until I could see what was there.

I slept better than I had done for a long time and woke up feeling as though someone had just changed my batteries. I had breakfast, packed up and decided to head out across the snow.

I walked for about five minutes and looked back to see how far I had travelled. I had made good progress, but something looked odd and I couldn't work out what. There was a slight fuzzy quality in the air, but this might have been due to any number of things. I was turning round to continue when I noticed what it was.

There were no marks in the snow showing where I had walked. No footprints or holes from my walking poles. No sign that I had ever touched the snow.

I looked in front of me again at the expanse of snow and then back again at where I had come. They looked identical. For the first time in a long while I became frightened. What was this? Was I still asleep and dreaming? I looked at my watch and took some comfort in the second hand sweeping slowly around the dial.

I knelt down and put my gloved hand in the snow. I felt the snow give way and form a soft hole as my hand pushed down into the clean powder. Then I took it out again. The snow was smooth, as if my hand had never been there. I looked at the glove and saw that there wasn't a single snowflake on it. I put my hand in again and this time took it out slowly. As I withdrew my hand I could actually see the snow rising back up again and reforming as my hand came out.

I fell backwards and lay there for a while, trying to think of some logical explanation for this behaviour. Nothing came to mind and I wondered if I had discovered something altogether new and unknown.

My initial fright had given way to the pure wonder of finding something so unique and magical. I started to experiment with the snow to see what, if any, effect I could have on it. I made a snow angel, but each time I moved my arms or legs the snow just popped back again as if I hadn't moved at all.

I wondered if I could eat the snow. I turned over and tried to take a mouthful of it, but my mouth just closed around air. I pushed my whole face down slowly to see what would happen. My face never touched anything; the snow moved away from me as my face moved down, almost as if my face were a magnet, repelling it.

I tried to pick some up to make a snowball, but my fingers couldn't close around anything; it was like trying to make a ball out of water.

What was going on? I looked out across the snow to the mountains on the other side. Did this strange snow stretch all the way across? Where did it start?

I got up and ran back the way I had come to see if I could find where my tracks had stopped. It wasn't that far – I was soon standing next to them and looking at the point where they were suddenly cut off. There was half a footprint in the snow where my track ended. I could see the heel mark, but the top half just wasn't there.

I took the shovel from my backpack and started digging at the point the footprint was broken off. I could dig as far as I liked on one side. On the other side, my spade could go in, but couldn't take any snow out. I dug down as far as the sea-ice, about four feet down. When I was finished, I was standing in a hole staring at a smooth, flat wall of snow in front of me. I could push into it a small way and even push myself out of it, but it always reformed itself.

I thought that if I was at one edge, whatever was causing this was somewhere in the other direction. I put my shovel away, put my backpack on and headed out again across the snow field.

I would see how far I had to go before my tracks started again.

Chapter 7

Bears

I walked forward, my mind racing, checking the snow every so often to see if my footprints stayed or not. After ten minutes there were still no marks in the snow. I wasn't paying much attention to my surroundings and I looked up to see a group of polar bears walking across the bay.

I stopped walking and stayed very still.

There were a couple of large bears with two cubs trotting along behind. They were only about a quarter of a mile away and seemed to be heading straight for me.

How could I have not noticed them before?

They didn't seem to be in any hurry, though, and there was something slightly unreal about the situation. I thought that if I started running, it might cause them to do the same, so I turned around slowly and started walking briskly back.

After a few steps I looked back to see what the bears were doing. The two larger bears had started running, leaving the cubs behind.

I quickly got out the flare pistol and loaded it, putting two more flares in my pocket, then started running as fast as I could. I knew that polar bears were not the fastest runners, but I was pretty sure they would be faster than me.

My only hope was that they would get tired and give up

the chase – I doubted I would make it to the mountains before them.

I turned round to look again. They were only about two hundred yards away. I stopped, pointed the flare gun over their heads and fired. The flare rose high above us and arced over the bears' heads. They stopped running and looked up at the flare as it passed overhead, then turned their heads to follow it as it fell back down, burning itself out before it hit the ground. They didn't seem to be scared of it in any way and they turned around again and looked straight at me.

I frantically reloaded the flare gun. I didn't really want to shoot directly at them unless I had no other choice, but couldn't think what else to do if they weren't frightened off by firing over their heads.

I was expecting them to start running towards me again, but instead they stood up on their back legs and started to sing.

I took a step back in shock. Was I imagining this?

They weren't growling or howling. There were notes moving up and down like a tune. I stood there, staring at them in amazement for a few moments, listening to these strange, otherworldly sounds.

The singing seemed to be affecting me in another way as well. My mind was suddenly full of images and patterns, swirling around like thoughts or memories. These weren't the half-formed images that exist in the back of your mind when you're awake; they were clear and real, as though I were watching a film.

There were images of snow and ice, the sea, mountains and wind.

Then there were voices inside my head describing specific images that were flashing through my mind.

Wind Over Mountain, the voice said.

Wind Over Sea, it added.

There were images of friends inviting me to dinner.

Follow the bears, the voice intoned.

I had no clue what was going on. Was I to believe that these bears were somehow communicating with me? That their singing was creating these responses in my head?

I was far more certain that I had somehow hit my head and was having very vivid visual and auditory hallucinations.

What was absolutely certain, though, was that I was not going to be following any bears anywhere. I dragged my eyes from this all-too-strange sight, turned back round again and carried on running. I could hear the singing stop and I looked back to see the bears running after me again. It seemed like the chase was on.

Every so often, one of them would start singing. I looked back and saw that the larger, male bear was the one chasing me and the female bear was the one standing up and singing. Then she would carrying on running for a bit before stopping to sing again.

So as well as being chased by a couple of polar bears, I

now had voices in my head. There were a few phrases that kept being repeated.

Wind Over Mountain.

Wind Over Sea.

Greetings.

The Sun Spirit needs you.

Follow the bears.

I carried on running.

Some way off, I could see the hole I had dug in the snow earlier; it gave me a point to aim for. I knew I didn't stand a chance against the bears wherever I was, but I was tiring and there was something slightly comforting about the thought of throwing myself into a small hole in this vast expanse of snow.

I didn't need to look behind me to see how close the bears were – I could hear the feet of the male bear as he thundered through the snow and it wasn't long before I could make out his heavy breathing. He sounded like he was just as exhausted as me, but he showed no signs of giving up.

The other bear was still breaking off from the running to sing occasionally. She must have fallen behind, because the voice in my head seemed further away now, fainter and more dream-like. I could still make out the words though, becoming more desperate and pleading.

Come, come. Don't leave.

The Sun Spirit needs you.

Stay, stay.

"Go, go. Run, run," I told myself.

The hole was still some way off. I thought I was going to make it when my backpack was suddenly ripped from my back and I was lifted off my feet and thrown into the air by one of the bear's paws.

I landed on my back and the bear was there, one massive paw weighing heavily on my chest, his face a couple of inches from mine, blasting me with a warm, foul, fishy stench.

He was trying to get his breath back, but managed to lift his head to sing a few notes.

Stay! The word echoed in my head.

I was finding it hard to breathe with his paw on me and I thought I might faint. I remembered that I was still holding the flare gun. In a daze, I raised it and fired straight at the bear.

There was a flash and I saw the flare bounce off the bear's shoulder and up into the air, leaving a dark stain on his white fur. He let out a mighty howl and leapt back.

His paw was off my chest and I quickly got to my feet and stumbled towards the hole.

I threw myself in and squatted down with my back against the snow catching my breath. I was trying to quickly reload the flare gun and looking out to see what the bear would do next.

He'd sat down where he was and he stayed there looking at me. Then he got up and ambled slowly towards me. He was limping slightly; he was in pain. I had the flare gun ready, but was shaking so much I doubted I would be able to hit him unless he was directly in front of me. But he didn't come right up to the hole and he stopped about twenty feet away and sat down again. Then he turned to see where the other bear was.

She was coming along at a slow run and the cubs were even further back, trying to catch up with their parents. She stopped when she got to the male bear and looked at him. When she saw his shoulder she started licking it. The male bear closed his eyes while she did this. If I were in the safety of my own home, watching this on the television, I'm sure I would have been charmed by this show of affection and bonding, but I was not at home and I wanted to know what was going to happen.

I shouted out to them, "leave me alone!"

The female bear stopped licking the other's wound and looked at me. Then she stood up and started singing again.

I straightened up in shock. I could hear the singing the same as before, but this time there were no images and no voices. It was just a bear making strange noises.

I wondered what had happened. Was it because I was now in my hole and back in the world of real snow, where footprints stayed where they were? Maybe this was also where singing bears couldn't get inside your head.

Was the communication limited to the strange snow? Was that why the bears hadn't tried to come any closer to me? Were they bound by this as well in some way and couldn't move outside it?

As I had nothing to lose, I thought I would test this idea. I gingerly got out of my hole and started walking away from the bears towards the mountain. I looked back with each step to see what they would do. The bears had stood up and moved a few paces forward, but had not passed the hole. They were watching me intently, and I could hear the female bear singing her heart out as I moved further away.

I stopped about fifty yards on and turned round. The female bear had stopped singing now. They were both moving around from side to side, as if unsure of which direction to go in, but they obviously weren't able to move forward in my direction.

I watched them with a growing sense of calm and relief. The bears soon stopped moving around and just sat down. The cubs had caught up by now and were running around everywhere, jumping on their parents and each other. I watched to see if they could cross the line, but they made no attempt to do so and I presumed they weren't able to either.

I lay back in the snow trying to make some sense of what had happened. My mind was clear and I could think freely now, but the more I thought about everything the less sense it made. I decided that the only thing that did make sense was that I was alive and that I was able to go home. I would have plenty of time to think about it as I walked back.

Then it dawned on me that I was still two days from the station and my backpack was a few yards from some

60

admittedly strange, but nevertheless very real and angry-looking bears.

I wasn't sure I'd be able to survive without my backpack, but I would have to get past the bears to retrieve it, or I would have to wait. The bears didn't look like they were going anywhere, though, and I wasn't sure how long I could just sit around waiting for them to leave before I froze to death.

We sat there looking at each other for about an hour. The cubs eventually got exhausted running around and went to their mother for a feed. I still had some film left in my pocket camera and I felt relaxed enough to get closer to them to take some photos.

The mother got up after feeding her cubs and started walking off. I sat very still and waited to see if the rest of the family would join her. The cubs trotted after her, but the male bear stayed where he was, lying down with his head on his paws, watching me and leaving me in no doubt that he would be there for as long as it took.

The longer I waited the more I would need to get my backpack to survive. By now it was late morning; I worked out that if I kept my breaks to a minimum I might be able to get back to the skidoo in a day and a half.

I had six energy bars and a packet of nuts and dried fruit in my coat.

I was thinking to myself, 'well, that's that'. This is the end of my adventure. Now all I had to do was walk for a day and a half with little food and somehow survive the night in sub-zero temperatures with nothing but my coat to keep me warm.

I got slowly to my feet and watched the bear stiffen and lift his head off his paws. I looked at him for a few moments. Then, because it felt like he'd won the contest, I saluted him before turning around and heading across the last bit of snow before the climb up the mountain.

I looked back from time to time as I walked up to see if the bear had got up and moved away, but I could see him, unmoving, getting smaller and smaller as I climbed higher and higher. By the time I got to the top I had lost sight of him, but I was pretty sure that if I went back to the place where I had last been able to just make him out, he would have still been there, waiting.

And then I was over the top and walking down the other side, leaving all the strangeness and mystery behind me. I didn't know what I was going to do about it when I got back. If I told people about it they might think I was mad and lock me up. Or worse; they would believe me and descend on the place to capture the bears and study everything, pulling it apart piece by piece until the mystery was solved and all the simple wonder had been destroyed.

Chapter 8

The Lizard on the Rock

I mulled over these and other thoughts as I descended. It was late afternoon; if I wanted to stand any chance of surviving the night, I would need to find somewhere to shelter from the worst of the cold. The temperature was already dropping and I knew very well how cold it was going to get.

To either side of the wide channel I was walking down there were areas where the mountainside hadn't been flattened so much by the lava flow. These areas were broken up by larger peaks and gullies where the rocks looked as though they had been hurled up through the body of the mountain as it heaved and split under the forces tearing it apart.

There was a ravine a short way down to my right that looked as if it might provide relief from the wind and the cold. The way into the ravine was partially blocked by boulders, which I thought would provide extra shelter. It seemed promising.

When I got closer, I saw that one of the rocks looked unusual. It was a different colour and had a more defined shape; one side was quite straight and the other side that I could see had a gentle curve. As I got nearer, I realised that it wasn't a rock at all; it must be man made. There were spots of colour – orange, rusting metal – that made it stand out from the mostly brown rocks around it.

I wondered if there had been some sort of research building up here that had been abandoned and, judging by what I could see, destroyed by a rock fall. It seemed an unlikely place for a research building, though, so then I thought that maybe an aeroplane had crash-landed a long time ago.

I quickened my pace with the excitement of what I might find. Soon I was jogging, my legs nearly falling over themselves as I ran down the slope.

And then I stopped.

I had seen a number of strange things over the last few days and months, but what faced me now was beyond anything I could have imagined.

Standing out from underneath the metal was a propeller. Not the propeller of an aeroplane, but quite clearly the propeller of a boat.

I was halfway up a mountain, staring at the back of a ship.

While I was trying to process this, I noticed that what I had previously thought were small patches of snow were actually the faded and peeling remnants of the last three letters of the ship's name: L U S.

My father's ship was *The Daedalus*. Was I looking at my father's ship?

I stumbled towards the ravine and started climbing up the jumble of rocks to the ship. As I made my way up I could see more of the hull, but the majority of the ship was still hidden from view.

When I got up to the ship, I pulled away some of the rocks near the lettering to reveal an 'A' and a 'D'. I could now see DALUS. I knew that if I removed more I would find the rest of the name.

I reached out and touched the lettering. I took one of my gloves off to feel the rough texture of the rusted metal and picked off some of the peeling paint to rub between my fingers so that I knew this was real.

I picked up a rock and banged on the steel, listening to the echo reverberate inside the ship.

Inside the ship. I stood there holding the rock in my hand. Was my father's body somewhere inside this ship?

I quickly scrambled up the last few rocks to where I could fully look into the ravine. The ship was lying on its left side. It was almost broken in two, the bow crumpled up like the nose of a paper aeroplane that had hit the ground. The whole front half had bent round as it tried to follow the course of the ravine. Not far from where I stood at the stern, the ship's bridge was almost completely destroyed; bent backwards by the wall of the ravine and then crushed by a huge slab of rock that must have fallen from one of the overhanging sections of the ravine, hundreds of feet up.

How does a ship get up a mountain? For the third time that day, I'd found something I was completely unable to explain. But however it got here, it must have been travelling at great speed. The collision brought down huge quantities of rock from the tall sides of the ravine. As well as covering the back of the ship and the entrance to the ravine, there were rocks strewn over the greater part of the ship. It was difficult to see a piece of metal that hadn't been bent or dented, either by the force of the initial collision or the impact of the falling rocks.

I wondered what happened to the crew as the ship careered into the ravine, and if any of them could have survived this.

I tried to imagine where my father might have been in the ship. Was he on the bridge, watching everything and trapped by the confined space? Was he on the deck, thrown off the ship as it sped towards this place? Or was he below decks, hurled around inside like a pea in a tin, unable to see what was going on?

It was hard thinking about these things, but I couldn't dwell on them for long. I was exhausted and hungry and beginning to shake with cold. My thoughts turned to food and shelter. I wondered if there were any tins of food still in the ship that might contain anything edible. There might also be blankets.

It was getting dark and the little light that was left in the day struggled to penetrate the gloom of the ravine. I had a small pocket torch, but it wouldn't last long and I had to get moving if I wanted to find anything to help me survive the night.

I clambered over the fallen rocks and boulders onto the stern and struggled up the sloping deck until I could make my way round the remains of the bridge and the rock that had crushed it. In front of the bridge was a large cabin with port holes, which extended halfway along the deck. I headed for a door a little further along the cabin that was half open and squeezed through, pausing to let my eyes adjust to the near darkness inside.

The cabin must have been the research area for the expedition; tables, chairs and smashed equipment were piled in heaps along the left-hand side of the tilted cabin. I let myself slide down the sloping floor and landed on a table, then scrambled over the furniture to some steps at the bridge end of the cabin.

The steps were almost horizontal because of the angle of the ship. I got out my torch, and gripping it in my teeth I crawled down the steps to the next level. Here, there were more steps going down to the engine room and a corridor lined with cabin doors leading to the bows of the vessel. It was difficult to say what was uppermost in my mind as I manoeuvred myself along the corridor: the need to find food and warmth, or the fear that some of the crew had been below decks when the ship crashed and that one of them would be my father.

I opened each cabin door I passed, the ones on the left falling open easily, due to the tilt of the ship, the ones on the right having to be pushed up to open them. I can't tell you how relieved I was that I didn't come across the remains of any crew members.

A door at the end of the corridor opened into the small area with three more doors. The one on my right-hand side was jammed shut, presumably by all the items in the room lying against it. I prayed this wasn't the food store. I opened the door in front of me and peered inside. It was the forward storeroom, full of an assortment of equipment thrown into a chaotic mess by the careering ship. I saw some smashed hurricane lamps, life jackets, some spare blankets, ropes and various other items, but no food.

I turned to the third door, lifting the handle to let the door fall open. I shone the torch into the dark space and let out a cry of thanks as I saw boxes and boxes of cans, spilt all over the far side of the store.

I slid into the room and started picking over the cans. Most of the labels had rotted away, so it was a bit of potluck what I found inside. The cold dry air had helped keep things in the best condition possible, considering the time they had been there, but a lot of what I found was dried out and inedible. I found some frozen baked beans that I could hack out with my knife, though, and I got a very pleasant surprise when I found a tin of peaches in syrup that were as good as if I had bought them yesterday. Inside one tin I even found a bar of chocolate that was still okay to eat. It was so cold, though, that I had to break it up with another tin and then suck the pieces until they melted in my mouth.

Once I'd eaten a little, I went back to the forward store

and searched among the items strewn around for anything that might be useful. I found some canvas knapsacks that looked like they could still be used, a few unbroken hurricane lamps still in their boxes, as well as paraffin and some matches. I had no expectation that the matches would strike or that the paraffin would burn and was amazed when I eventually managed to get them all working so that I could enjoy the rest of my evening feast with a little more light than that produced by my fading torch.

I ate until I couldn't eat anything else, then I got some mattresses and blankets from the cabins closest to me and put the mattresses together to make a rough level surface in the sloping compartment before covering myself in as many blankets as I could and falling fast asleep.

I had an uneasy night. My dreams were full of wild images from the day and from my own mind trying to make sense of everything. The bears were there, sitting down, talking about the stars. I wanted to join in their conversation, but when I got closer, they dissolved into snow that whirled around me in a furious storm of white that never touched me, but lifted me up and up, away from the ground and into the bright blue air above.

My father's ship was sailing majestically through the sky on giant wings and I was flying behind it. The bears had joined me and were gliding along beside me. I was telling them the ship was named Daedalus after the father of Icarus. I told them how Daedalus was a great inventor and had made his son a wonderful pair of wings so that he could fly. But he flew too high and the sun melted the wax used to bind the wings together, and Icarus fell to his death. The bears looked at me sadly and moved away asking me to follow them, but I said that I had to stay with my father. They pleaded with me to come with them and told me to look at the wings of the ship. I looked and saw that the wings were made of wax and that they were starting to melt in the bright sunshine.

I waved madly at the men on the decks and shouted at them to look at the wings, but they didn't see me. I sped closer and tried to reach the bridge so I could warn the captain. The wings were starting to unravel and the ship began to fall from the sky. I was nearly up to the bridge and I could see the captain. Next to the captain was my father and my father was…

I woke up with a start, sweating.

Was that my father? What had he been doing? I shook myself fully awake and told myself that it was just a dream and that I needed to eat and leave as soon as I could.

I turned the torch on so I could see my watch. There were still two hours until dawn. I could feel the cold seeping into my body. Even though I had more protection here, I knew I needed to get back to the station as soon as possible.

I didn't want to set off until it had started to get light. I also thought I couldn't leave the ship without looking anywhere else I could get into, to see if there was any trace of my father or the rest of the crew.

I lit one of the hurricane lamps and ate a breakfast of peaches and frozen baked beans. There was enough food to last for weeks, so I filled one of the knapsacks with a few days rations and tied a couple of blankets to it in case I had to spend another night in the open. I also found crampons, which I knew I would need for the next climb.

I walked back along the passageway until I came to the steps that went up to the research cabin and down to the engine room. Leaving the knapsack by the stairs, I picked up the hurricane lamp and shuffled down the steps to the engine room, headfirst. I was afraid of what might be revealed as I shone the light into the space, but there was nothing. No one had been in the engine room when the ship crashed.

Turning round, I crawled back along the steps, wondering what might have happened to the crew. At the top of the steps I picked up the knapsack, hoisted it onto my back and made my way up the steps back into the research cabin.

I sat there for a while, looking at the steps leading up into the bridge. These had been squashed and contorted and I wasn't sure if I would be able to even get into the bridge, but I had to try. Holding the lamp in one hand, I pulled myself along the handrails with my other hand, trying to squeeze along the crumpled space that used to be a stairway.

At one time the steps would have led up to a small platform before the door into the bridge. All of this was gone. The door was ripped from its hinges and the opening crushed to the extent that a child wouldn't have been able to get through.

I reached up and held the hurricane lamp inside, then squeezed my head in as best I could.

I cried out and let go of the lamp.

I had seen a hand.

The ship wasn't empty. Here was a crew member and this is where they had died. The reality hit me and I nearly fell back down the sloping stairway.

For a moment I was in complete darkness, but the lamp had smashed against something and the paraffin caught alight, casting everything in an eerie, flickering glow.

I looked back into the hole. In the dim light I saw two arms, but the rest of the body was hidden under the twisted and crushed metal of the bridge.

The two arms were reaching towards me, the hands clasped around an object. It was a simple, smooth, grey ball and it was being held out to me as if being presented.

I was staring at the ball, trying to work out what it might be, when I noticed the rings hanging loosely on the frozen, dried-up fingers that encased it. There was a plain gold band on the wedding finger of the left hand, but on one of the fingers of the right hand there was a signet ring. I looked closer at the design on the ring. It was of a lizard on a rock. My heart started racing and my breathing quickened as though I was running out of air.

You'll understand why, if you look at the rings your mother

wears. She has a ring just like the one I was looking at. It was our mother's, your grandmother's. It was the only thing she kept to remember the man who gave it to her. The man whose remains I was looking at now.

My father.

I admit that I cried while I held on to my dead father's hands. I didn't have much time, though, as the light from the fire started by the lamp was getting brighter and the smoke thicker. The fire must have caught hold of some of the dried, wooden structure and was burning up anything it could find.

It was the most difficult thing I've had to do in a long time, but I had to leave my father where he was. I gently tried to open his hands to take the grey ball, but they were frozen solid and I had to prise each finger off before the object dropped into my hand. It seemed incredibly heavy at first, but I must have imagined it, because it was easy enough to move and put in my pocket. I would have time to examine it later and try to find out why anything could be so important that my father would be holding onto it while the ship was being crushed.

I carefully took the signet ring from my father's dried-up finger before climbing back down the steps to the main cabin.

It was just after dawn and the first of the morning rays were stealing into the ravine, providing enough light for me to leave the other hurricane lamp. I slowly climbed out of the ship the way I had come and stood there for a while, looking at the smoke rising from the area around the bridge. I doubted that it would consume the entire vessel, but it might destroy the bridge and everything in it, including my father.

I felt that I should say something, but I didn't know what words to use, or what words would be right.

I built a small cairn and sang one of the few hymns I could remember, 'I vow to thee my country'. My lonely song sounded out across the mountains and echoed down the ravine, coming back to me out of the darkness like the voice of a stranger.

It did little to settle me. What did all this mean? How was any of it possible?

I turned all these thoughts and everything else that I had seen over and over in my mind as I made the long, cold walk back across the mountains.

It was two days before I got to the skidoo. I was frozen and exhausted, and although I was in slightly better shape when I got back to the station than the last time, I still needed to go straight to the hospital. And, as you saw, I still managed to lose part of another finger.

In the days it took me to recover I came to a decision. I had found my father's ship and I had found my father. But I had also found a mystery; a mystery so strange that I knew I would have to go back to try and solve it.

I knew that the snow, the bears and my father's ship were all linked in some way. And I couldn't get rid of the idea that the ball my father had been holding was an important part of the same puzzle.

So, Dear Boy, that's why I've sent it to you.

It's my insurance policy to make sure I return in one piece.

Look after it. I'm going to talk to some bears.

Your loving uncle

Henry

Chapter 9

Head

I put the letter down thinking of the strange things Uncle Digit had written about.

Did all this really happen, or was he just writing an adventure beyond anything that he'd ever told me before?

Mum came in to see how I was getting on. Although I doubted she would believe anything in it, I gave her the letter. She sat down opposite me at my bedroom table and I waited patiently until she had read it.

Once or twice I caught her trying to suppress a giggle, but then as she got to the last few pages, she let out a small gasp of surprise. Her mouth closed tight and her eyes became harder, staring intently at the pages.

She remained quite still for a minute when she had finished, before almost absentmindedly handing the pages to me without raising her head.

I took them and folded them up, placing them carefully on the table between us.

"What do you think, Mum?"

There was an uncomfortable pause before she lifted her head to look at me.

"What do I think?" she said with barely concealed anger. "I think your uncle's gone too far this time."

"Too far?"

"I know he desperately wants to find our father, to have some sort of closure to end all of the not knowing. But pretending to find him and inventing a whole fantasy around it is just too much. It's not fair on you, or on me and probably not fair on himself either."

I didn't know what to say and watched her as she sat there thinking, biting her lip.

"I suppose I didn't realise just how desperately he wanted to find him," she said eventually in a calmer voice.

"Do you think about your father?" I asked her.

"Not in the way your uncle does. My mother was still pregnant with me when our father left, so I have no memory of him. Your uncle was five, though. He remembers spending time with him, remembers him leaving and, more importantly, remembers him not coming back."

"I still remember bits about Dad," I said quietly, "even though I was very little."

Mum's face collapsed a bit and she came round to give me a hug.

We sat there not saying anything for a while, then we talked about how much we missed my dad. Mum brought out the family photos and, as we went through them, she told me things about my dad she hadn't mentioned before. It was still hard for her to talk about him, but she carried on and I could see that it got easier as more stories came out and she was laughing and crying at the same time. It felt good for both of us and I realised that we probably wouldn't have done this if it hadn't been for Uncle Digit writing about his adventures.

We waited to hear from him again, but nothing arrived. The summer holidays came and went and the school routine started again. I was in my room scribbling down notes for some stories instead of doing homework. I heard the phone ring and a few minutes later Mum called up.

"Finn! Can you come down, please?"

I quickly picked up my crutches and went downstairs to the hall where she was standing patiently, holding the phone out to me and smiling.

"It's your uncle."

I took the handset from her eagerly and held it to my ear. "Hello?" I said.

"Hello, Finn." The voice was very crackly, but there was no mistaking it. "Can you hear me? It's not a very good line."

"I can hear you fine!" I said, shouting a little. "Are you alright?"

"I've never felt better," he chuckled. "Seriously."

"Did you go back again?"

"Yes, I went back."

"What happened?" I said, unable to contain my excitement.

"I've got so much to tell you. I couldn't possibly tell you everything over the phone."

"Oh! Okay," I said, trying not to sound too disappointed.

"But when are we going to see you?"

"You won't have long to wait. I'll be with you in four or five days."

"Really!" I looked up at Mum, who seemed just as excited as I was.

"Yes, really. I just wanted to ring and let you know before I left here. I've got a long drive ahead of me, so I need to go now. Look after yourself, Sport."

"Okay. I will. Bye."

"Well, that's a lovely surprise, isn't it?" Mum said.

I was still bubbling with excitement when we sat down for supper. I was talking about everything that I wanted to do when Uncle Digit arrived and teased Mum about how many fingers he was going to come back with this time.

She laughed, then pulled faces at me to show that she still disapproved of my name for her brother and was not impressed with the idea of him coming back with even fewer fingers than he had already been reduced to.

I was up in my room again a few days later when I heard the front door go. Mum's little squeak of joy was enough to tell me that it was my uncle. I could hear them talking and at one point I heard Mum gasp, but then he was bounding up the stairs and into my room.

"Dear Boy, I can't tell you how good it is to see you again. Look, I've got my digits back!"

He held up his hands and I saw that all of his fingers were

there again. All the questions I had been burning to ask about his letter vanished in a puff of astonishment.

"But, how...?" I asked.

"I'll tell you later," he said, smiling at me. "You won't be disappointed."

"Wow, you really are Uncle Digit now."

"Uncle Digit?" he said, his usual non-stop flow of speech and movement suddenly halted.

"Yes, that's what I call you. Mum doesn't like it, but I was hoping you would."

"Uncle Digit. Well, yes. Actually, it's more suitable now than you can possibly imagine."

"It could be Lord Digit if you prefer," I said, bowing my head.

He bowed from the waist with a flourish.

"Lord Digit of the Frozen Wastes and Blasted Plains, Conqueror of the Ravaged Peaks and Guardian of the Stars, at your service."

We both laughed.

"Not really my style, though, don't you think?" he added.

"No. Uncle Digit it is then," I said definitively.

His eyes searched the room. "You still have that grey ball I sent you to look after for me, don't you?" he asked.

"Of course," I said. "I keep it near me all the time. It's in the drawer of my bedside table there."

Uncle Digit went and got the ball out, then pulled up a

chair and sat down at the table opposite me.

"Does it feel odd when you pick it up?" I asked him as he sat there looking at the ball.

He looked up at me. "What do you feel?" he asked me.

"It's like I'll never be able to move it," I said. "Then, it just comes up in my hands. It sort of calms me as well when I'm holding it. Do you feel the same when you pick it up?"

"Yes. It's strange, isn't it?"

He sat there looking at it. Then he moved it around slowly in his hands, a look of almost child-like surprise and wonder breaking over his grizzled face. He laughed softly to himself and mumbled words like "amazing" and "incredible".

I wondered if his injuries and all the time he'd spent in the cold on his own had been too much, even for him.

"Are you all right?" I asked him gently.

He stopped turning the ball over and looked at me, his expression still showing the amazement he seemed to hold for the object.

"Do you know how many times I've held this ball in my hands, staring at it, trying to work out what it was and why it was so important to my father?"

"Do you know what it is?"

"I do now. But I don't think your grandfather knew what it really was, or he might not have taken it in the first place."

"He took it?" I said.

"Yes, he did. And I have to take it back."

"Back? Where?" I asked, confused. "Are you going to take it back to the ship?"

"No, not the ship. I have to take it to its rightful owner."

"But, how did you find out who it belongs to after all this time?"

"Because I met them." He was smiling now and obviously enjoying the sense of mystery he was building up and the look of bewilderment on my face.

"You met them?"

"Yes."

"But where?"

"You read my letter, didn't you?" he asked, narrowing his eyes at me, but still smiling.

"Of course I did, loads of times."

He was obviously waiting for me to come to some conclusion.

"You mean it belongs to the bears?" I said, doubting the words even as they left my mouth.

Uncle Digit laughed. "No, not the bears. Look, it's going to take a bit of explaining. It's probably best if I just tell you what happened when I went back."

"Okay," I said, settling down for the story.

But the story didn't come. He sat staring down at the table, as though he were struggling to find the right words.

"Tell me," he said, looking up. "Did you believe everything that I wrote in my letters?"

"Well…" I reached for the right words. "It's all rather incredible."

"It is, isn't it?"

"Mum got very cross. She thought it was wrong to make up stories about something that was so important to your life."

"And she would be right, if I had made it up. But I didn't."

"So, all of the things you wrote about actually happened?"

"Yes."

I let that sink in, not quite knowing what to think anymore.

"Before I tell you anything else, I need to show you something. Something that will prove that everything I wrote is real."

"Okay," I said.

He'd stopped smiling now and was looking at me intently. "But this is going to be hard for you. When you see it, you'll appreciate that it's not something I would share with anyone else. One day your mother might know and understand, but for now, it's just you. Can you handle that?"

Normally, the build-up to his stories created a heightened sense of anticipation in me, but his tone was deadly serious. For once, I found myself feeling tense and nervous at what might follow.

"Yes," I said, a little uncertainly.

"It's not just my fingers that have been put back together again. I had a really bad accident."

"What happened?" I asked.

"Well, everything, really. I fell through the sea-ice."

My eyes widened. "Wow," was all that came out.

Uncle Digit sighed. "I don't remember much, but when I woke up I was like this."

"But you look completely normal," I said. "I can't see anything different."

"You can't see anything, no, but I am very different."

"In what way?" I asked.

"You'll see. Just remember that whatever happens, I'm fine and you're not imagining anything. Everything is real, okay?"

"Yes," I said.

"It's a bit scary, but try to breathe and stay calm."

"Okay," I said, now definitely on the unrelaxed side of staying calm.

Uncle Digit held his hands up to the sides of his head with one hand on each ear.

"Oh, and try not to scream," he added casually.

"Right. Don't scream," I replied.

There was the softest of hisses, then he picked his head up in his hands and placed it on the table in front of me.

I sat back as far as I could and tried really hard not to scream. I looked from the head to the body and back to the head again. Then I stared at the place his head had come from. There was no sign of blood or bone or anything that you might expect to be there. It was as smooth as polished metal or glass and it shimmered and seemed to flow almost like liquid.

Part of me wanted to go over and touch it and part of me wanted to get away from there as fast as possible.

"But... What..." The words wouldn't come. I was finding it hard to take it in.

Then the shock finally hit me. Uncle Digit was there in front of me, in two pieces.

"Mum!" I shouted. "Mum!"

"What is it?" Mum's alarmed voice came from downstairs.

"It's... It's..." I was still having difficulty speaking and then I suddenly blurted out, "his head's come off!"

I heard Mum sigh. "Have you broken one of your toys again?" she said impatiently. "Can't your uncle fix it?"

I looked at Uncle Digit's head on the table. He was smiling, but not saying anything.

"No, Mum, it's not one of my toys. It's Uncle Digit: his head comes off!"

Mum started walking up the stairs. "I do wish you'd stop calling him that! I think we can all agree your uncle's off his head, but anything else would be too much, even for him."

Uncle Digit winked at me, then his head gently rose off the table and settled back onto his neck with not the slightest mark to indicate that it had ever been separated.

Mum's head appeared round the door. "Now what's all this nonsense?" she said, looking at both of us.

I was speechless.

"Close your mouth, Finn; your uncle's not a dentist."

I shut my mouth.

Mum was looking from one of us to the other. "Well?" she said finally. "Anybody?"

Uncle Digit turned to face Mum. "I think the shock of seeing my new fingers made him rather imaginative."

"Yes, I suppose it is a bit of a shock, but nothing to get alarmed about. I think it's wonderful what they can do nowadays. Now, why don't you two boys go out and get some fresh air for an hour or so before lunch?"

"Excellent idea," Uncle Digit said, positively beaming.

"Is it?" I said, with just a small note of panic in my voice.

"What's the matter? You normally can't wait to get outside with your uncle. You haven't been frightening him with your stories, have you, Henry?"

"No. But I promise to scare him witless by the time we come back."

I couldn't help feeling there might be some truth to that.

Once Mum had closed the door, Uncle Digit turned and faced me, looking concerned.

"I'm really sorry, Finn. I know that was a lot for you to take in at once, but I needed you to see it so that you would believe everything else I'm going to tell you."

"So, that wasn't a trick?"

"No, of course not. I can do it again if you like."

"No! Please, I like your head where it is."

Uncle Digit laughed. "So do I."

"So, your head can come off?"

"Yes."

"And you have new fingers?"

"Yes."

"And this didn't all happen in some fancy new hospital?"

"No."

"Okay then. I suppose we should go out and you can tell me how this all happened."

"Exactly. Now come on." He handed me my crutches. "I'll race you downstairs."

"Very funny."

I thought that as soon as I got in my chair and we were outside, I would be asking a million questions, or Uncle Digit would be pouring out his story, but we were both silent as he pushed me along.

My mind was a whirl and I didn't know where to start. I wanted Uncle Digit to just talk, to explain what had happened, to calm me down and reassure me everything was all right, but he wasn't saying anything. This frustrated me until I realised that he was probably letting me work things through until I felt ready to ask him something.

I stayed quiet and we carried on slowly and silently to the river and started along the towpath.

After a while, Uncle Digit bent down to look round at my face. "Are you okay, Small Fry?"

He hadn't called me that since I was little. It felt nice to hear him say it now; it was comforting, like he was tucking me into bed and kissing me good night.

"Yes," I said, looking up at him. "I was just letting things settle down."

"I hoped you were. How are you feeling about carrying on?"

"Does it get any scarier?" I asked.

"What? Scarier than your uncle taking his head off?"

I laughed.

"Well," he carried on, "It's certainly strange, but I don't think it gets scarier."

"It doesn't matter; I want to hear it all."

"Excellent."

He pushed me gently along by the river and I sat back and closed my eyes, listening as he told me everything that had happened to him.

Chapter 10
Talking to Bears

The hospital was at the edge of a small logging town. From my window I could see out to the forests that continued in unbroken waves of green until height, water or the cold prevented anything from growing.

It was grey and uninviting. The snows would start soon and it would be difficult to get in or out of the station. I knew I needed to leave soon.

The hospital was used to dealing with injuries from these cold, mountainous regions and I was looked after well and efficiently.

It only took me a few days to recover from the frostbite and fatigue, but I had to wait for another week before I could hitch a ride out on the next supply helicopter, so I was well rested by the time I left.

It was good to catch up with the research team again at the station. They made fun of me and thought I was a little mad going out on my own again. Part of me agreed with them, but the other part couldn't wait to leave, and I packed up what I needed and got everything ready for my trip.

It was another day or two before there was a good break in the weather, then I got back on the skidoo and set out at sunrise.

It was starting to feel a bit like going to work, though. I left the skidoo and started walking up the mountain for the third time. The wind and the freezing cold hit me and I asked myself why was I doing all this again?

I had found my father and his ship, but what could possibly explain everything else that I had seen? And if something could explain it, did I really want to know what it was?

I suppose that was the key: the 'knowing' and 'not knowing' that drove me on. I needed to find out more, to uncover secrets and open boxes never opened before.

It was nearly dark on the evening of the third day from the station when I got to the ship. The fire had done little damage and the stern of the ship was untouched.

I stood for a few minutes by the small cairn of stones I had built to remember my father, then climbed back on board and down to the cabins, making myself as comfortable as possible in the storeroom and eating my rations with some peaches and chocolate before going to sleep.

My father's remains were with me in this ship. This unsettled me and comforted me in turns. I had a restless sleep, but had no more dreams of bears and flying ships.

I started off at first light, full of doubt. I was heading out to try and find some fully grown polar bears so that I could 'talk' to them and find out what they wanted with me. It didn't sound very promising.

I had been turning everything over in my mind. The only

thing that made me believe there was any hope was that the bear hadn't killed me when he had the chance.

If it wasn't for the fact that I had just spent the night in a boat halfway up a mountain, I would be tempted to believe that I had hallucinated everything.

I made good progress and got over the mountain and down the other side by late afternoon. As I got closer to the shoreline I could see one of the bears lying down near the hole I had dug.

It looked like the larger, male bear. At first I thought he was on his own, but when he saw me coming he got up and a smaller white bundle erupted from the snow close by and ran around him. It didn't look like one of the cubs; it was too big.

I realised it was an Arctic fox. Its presence, so close to the polar bear, added to the strangeness of the scene and calmed me: if the bear wasn't attacking the fox, it seemed less likely that it would attack me. Was that why the fox was there? Was it meant to reassure me?

The bear watched the fox for a few moments, then tried to swipe it with a paw. The fox easily avoided it, but it stopped running around and sat a little way off from the bear. They both sat there watching me as I headed towards them.

I walked as far as the hole and sat down with my legs dangling over the edge, safe in the knowledge that they couldn't come any closer. I was waiting for something, some sign that it was okay for me to continue, to try and talk to these creatures.

The bear stood up and started singing. As before, it had no effect on me outside the snow field. The fox looked at him and scratched one of his ears. It made some noises at the bear in a high, whimpering voice. The bear stopped singing and looked at the fox before moving his head closer, baring his teeth and growling rather loudly. The fox leapt back and turned round a few times before lying down on the ground some way off, looking from me to the bear.

The bear had stopped singing and was sitting there, his head slightly on one side, staring at me with what looked very much like a scowl on his face.

I dropped down into the hole and leant forward onto the snow on the other side so that I knew I was within the snow field.

"Hello," I said, rather pointlessly.

The fox looked at the bear and sang in his high-pitched tones.

Now you can speak. The human can hear you now, a voice inside my head clearly intoned.

The bear snapped round at him.

Quiet. Wind Over Mountain does not need Eater of Dirt to explain things, said a slightly deeper voice in my head.

The bear turned to look at me and continued singing.

Wind Over Mountain sends greetings from the Sun Spirit and demands that Burning Light come, said the bear's voice.

The fox looked up.

Not 'demands'. The Sun Spirit 'asks' that the human comes. The human must come freely.

Wind Over Mountain does not see the difference.

It looked like they were going to start an argument.

"Why should I come?" I asked quickly.

Burning Light will come because Burning Light is asked, the bear said.

"Burning Light? Is that me?"

Wind Over Mountain does not see anyone else.

"Why do you call me Burning Light?" I asked.

You hurt Wind Over Mountain with burning light, the bear said and he looked at his shoulder, where I could still make out the shape of the wound I had inflicted in his fur.

"I'm sorry I hurt you," I said. "I thought you were trying to kill me."

Wind Over Mountain does not understand 'sorry'.

"I mean that I wish that I hadn't hurt you."

But Burning Light did hurt Wind Over Mountain. How can Burning Light change this?

"Burning Light can't change this," I admitted.

But Burning Light will come, Wind Over Mountain insisted.

I paused, but I had already made my mind up.

"I suppose I will," I said.

I got out of the hole and stood on the other side, in the

impossible snow, looking from the bear to the fox. The bear turned around and started walking across the snow field.

The fox waited for me to move and then trotted along beside me. We walked without speaking for a while, with only the wind breaking the peaceful stillness of the bay.

"So, you're called Wind Over Mountain?" I asked the bear after some time in an attempt to break the silence.

Yes.

"The last time there was another bear and some cubs."

The dark times come. Wind Over Sea is with the young.

"Wind Over Sea? Wind Over Mountain and Wind Over Sea," I repeated to myself, thinking that they were good names for bears. "I heard you saying these before, but I didn't know they were your names."

There wasn't any response so I turned to the fox.

"What do you call yourself?"

We don't have names, the fox replied.

"But I thought I heard Wind Over Mountain call you something before."

Eater of Dirt, sang the bear, the disdain clear in his voice.

The fox managed to look uncomfortable.

"Do you really eat your own dirt?" I asked him.

You eat what you can out here, the fox said.

The bear turned his head. *Wind Over Mountain never eats dirt.*

"Why don't you give yourselves names?" I asked the fox.

What for? You don't meet much round here and what you do meet either wants to eat you, or you want to eat it.

"But the bears give themselves names."

Bears think they're poets, the fox said, making a face as though he'd just eaten something unpleasant. *They're all called 'Wind Over Mountain' or 'Moonlight On The Snow' or something like that.*

It didn't look like he wanted to carry on the conversation, so we continued on again in silence. The complete unreality of walking and talking with a couple of wild animals was fading, and I began to try and make sense of what was happening to me.

The images appearing in my head when the fox had last spoken had been about bears singing to the stars, but the words that I heard in relation to them were, 'bears think they're poets'. My mind was somehow translating the clear dream-like images into words and phrases that I could understand. But how was this dream-speak even possible? How could something be getting inside my head to do this?

I wondered if the same thing was happening to the animals; that my words were somehow being translated into images and maybe even sounds that carried meaning for them.

We carried on walking across the snow for what seemed like ages, but must have only been half an hour or so. The wind was blowing in from the sea and I could taste the salt in the air. I watched as the gusts whipped the bottom of my trousers around my boots and marvelled again at the fact that it had no effect on the snow, which just lay smooth and flat in front of and behind us.

I had been trying to chat to the fox, but he didn't seem to know much about what was going on and why I was needed. I wanted to find out anything else I could before we got to our destination, so I caught up with the bear and walked beside him for a while.

"Why does the Sun Spirit need me?" I asked him.

Wind Over Mountain does not know this, he replied.

"Who is the Sun Spirit?"

The Sun Spirit is the spirit of the sun, he said in a manner that implied there was no need to ask any further questions.

"How do you know this?" I ventured.

How do you not know this? the bear asked back.

I was at a loss for what to say.

The Sun Spirit holds the Light of the Sun. There is no one else who can do this, Wind Over Mountain continued.

"The Light of the Sun?"

Indeed.

"It will be interesting to see this."

You cannot see this.

"No? Why not?"

The Light has been stolen.

Chapter 11
Dark Star

By now it was approaching dusk and we were only about halfway across the snow field. It would be dark soon, but no one seemed to be in any hurry.

Suddenly both the bear and the fox stopped. They were staring intently at a point in the distance, away to the left-hand side of the great sweeping curve of the mountain range.

In the fading light I could just see a dark spot on the snow moving in our direction. I looked over at the bear.

"You know what that is?" I asked him.

Yes. Wind Over Mountain will stay and fight.

"Fight?" I asked. "What is it?"

It is...

There were images, but the dream-speak could find no words to describe them. Images of destruction and emptiness; a darkness so complete that I almost lost my balance. It was like I was on the edge of a black hole, staring into a place where nothing could exist.

As the dark form came closer, I could distinguish three separate shapes within the swirling blackness. I looked around me at the expanse of empty snow. We were as close to the middle as was possible and there was nowhere to run.

After another minute or so it was possible to make out

two bears pulling a writhing form behind them. They looked like polar bears, but were completely black.

I looked at Wind Over Mountain, but he didn't look like he was going to talk anymore and was focused solely on the approaching figures.

I turned to the fox. "Are they bears?"

They look like bears to me, came the quick response.

Wind Over Mountain raised his head.

They were bears before, but now they are just shells of bears, full of fear and hate. They are not bears.

The shapes were getting closer. Indeed, they looked as though they were full of fear and hate. They also looked as though they would be able to tear me apart with ease, and I had the strongest desire to run as fast as I could in the opposite direction.

"How can you hope to fight them?" I asked.

The fox didn't seem keen on staying to fight either. He was whimpering and moving around in an agitated way, as if he were trying to run away but was somehow tied to the spot.

The Sun Spirit will protect us, Wind Over Mountain said.

"Really?" I looked around, wondering where or when this mysterious being would appear to save us.

I turned back to look at the bears hurtling towards us and doubted that any help would arrive in time. Wind Over Mountain looked like he was getting ready to charge. The fox had quietened down and was also steeling himself for whatever lay ahead.

I had taken out my flare gun as the only weapon available to me. The oncoming bears and the writhing dark shape were only a couple of hundred yards away. There were only moments left before they were on us.

Then I felt it.

It was as if someone had thrust their hands inside my head and was scooping everything up, trying to separate my being strand by strand, unravelling me into individual components.

I dropped the flare gun and fell to my knees, tearing at my hair.

My senses, my thoughts, my hopes and visions, and every memory I ever had were being dragged out and ransacked, laid out like items in a shop window, being picked over, selected, or discarded by whatever was doing this.

Outside the whirling chaos that was going on inside my head, everything was suddenly motionless.

The world had frozen in an instant and there was a silence as if I had gone completely deaf. Time had stopped and I was able to look around at every detail.

I saw Wind Over Mountain, caught in a moment as he raised himself up, ready to charge at the oncoming bears. The fox had lowered his head and looked as though he were about to leap up onto the attackers.

Each hair on the black bears stood out clearly and I could see the foam that had flown from their mouths as they charged forward lying suspended in the air. I could see their eyes, not focused on anything, but staring wildly in different directions as if they were trying to escape from the blackness that was pushing them forward, expelling them onward.

And I could sense the blackness watching me, searching me and I knew that this was the presence inside me: a thousand fingers sifting and pulling at the threads of my life.

I was drawn sharply back into what was going on inside me. The countless thoughts and feelings that had been rushing around had stopped. I saw one image: my father's dead hands offering me the ball inside the ship. The image was being shown to me, not by myself, but by the presence inside my head. It was this then; the small grey ball I had taken from my father. This was what they were looking for. I felt the presence grow stronger and more forceful. I had to give it to them. I had no choice. I had to show them where it was and all this would end. All I had to do was think about it and it would be over. If I didn't, it would slowly invade every part of me until there was nothing of myself left. I would become like the black bears, unable to control the slightest movement by myself.

I was desperately focusing on anything else I could think of: assignments I had been on; films I had seen; football matches I had been to. I could sense the presence circling around the memories of the grey ball, showing me anything it could find that it thought might be connected. I knew it would only be a matter of time before it found out that I didn't have it and that it was somewhere in a boy's bedroom in England.

I concentrated on the image it already had of my father's hands around the ball. I used it as a shield to hide every other thought I had. I made that one image fill my mind, occupying every space until there was nothing else but that moment. It became as real as if I were standing there again, looking in on the crushed remains of my father, his hands offering me the ball. There were the smells of the ship and the burning oil from the lamp I had dropped. There was the flickering light and the faint crackling sounds as the fire ignited bits of timber. I could feel the steps beneath my feet. When I reached out and took the ball from my father's hands again, it felt exactly as it had done before.

I held the ball up and looked at it. I turned it over and over in my hands wondering again what it was and why someone or something would want it so much. I was holding it in my fingers, just staring at it, willing it to somehow tell me its secrets. Slowly the greyness of the surface started to give way and there was light shining from inside the ball. The light grew quickly until it became a blinding white that expelled everything else around me. The inside of the ship disappeared and the light continued to grow until there was nothing else but an incandescent brightness, filling and cleansing the world inside me.

The presence inside my head was gone, together with the ship and the ball. I was back on the snow again and the real world outside rushed in.

The black bears came to a sudden stop ten feet in front of Wind Over Mountain and the fox. They were panting and snarling and snapping at each other but making no attempt to attack.

Wind Over Mountain had dropped back onto his feet and the fox was standing still. Next to them, floating a few inches above the snow, was a white cylinder about eight feet tall, which had appeared as if from nowhere.

Was this the Sun Spirit that Wind Over Mountain said would come?

Nothing happened for a few moments and then the dark shape flowed out from behind the bears. It drifted slowly, a malign black cloud with arms of thick dark smoke coiling from its formless body. Some of the arms glowed with a red light that quickly grew out of the ends to became long red tendrils of fire that turned and snaked like whips ready to lash.

The shape drew closer to Wind Over Mountain and the fox, tendrils raised up, ready to strike. The next instant the white cylinder moved so quickly it looked as if it had just materialised in front of the dark shape. It had produced bright blue tendrils of its own that engaged each of the red tendrils. The pair were locked together and almost motionless, apart from the blue and red lines that were moving around slowly, disengaging and re-engaging as they pushed and probed for weaknesses and openings. Each time they touched there were bright flashes of pure energy. The force that these generated created a wind that built up and swirled around everyone, making it difficult to stand.

I started running. I couldn't tell in which direction, just anywhere away from what was happening behind me. I could hear the bear's deep tones and the fox's high yelps over the roar of the wind, but no images or words came. I looked back and could just make them out running after me through the whirling snow. The black mass and the white cylinder were starting to spin around each other and had become a blur lit up by bursts of lightning that flashed as they fought.

The next time I looked back, I could see that the bear had stopped running. The fox was a bit nearer, sniffing the ground ahead of him. He looked up at me and barked something out. I shouted above the wind. "I can't understand what you're saying anymore, but it doesn't matter. Look at them! What can we do to help? This is their fight. I don't care if your Sun Spirit needs me. I'm getting as far away from them as possible."

I turned away and started running again.

Then the snow gave way. My boots went straight through the powder, pulling me down into the sea below.

There was the instant shock of being in freezing water. Then there was just darkness.

Chapter 12

The Keeper

I woke up and opened my eyes.

Everything was white. Was I still on the snow? I couldn't be on the snow. I had no clothes on, but I felt warm.

I was lying on a small platform. I thought that I could just make out a ceiling and walls. Everything was so uniformly white that it seemed to extend forever.

I wondered if I was dead.

There was a quick movement and the white cylinder appeared in front of me. I hadn't had much time to take it in before, but I could see now that it was not quite a cylinder; it had more shape to it. There was a vague head and small shoulders at the top and curves on the sides. The curves protruded slightly and might have been arms that tapered as they lengthened to the more rounded end of the object. It was hovering a few inches above the ground.

I tried to make out any features, but I could see no eyes or mouth or any variation to the surface to indicate a bodily function.

I tried to get up.

It would be better if you stayed lying down.

The voice inside my head was crystal clear and the images that accompanied it were quick and sharp. I don't know whether they had chosen the voice I would hear or if I had chosen the voice myself, but it was the calm, reassuring voice of a mother setting the world to rights after everything had just fallen apart.

I lay back down.

"Who are you?" I asked.

There was no immediate response.

"Wind Over Mountain calls you the Sun Spirit."

I am The Keeper of the Sun Heart of the Golden System and Provider of Light to The First of the Crescent Worlds that lie beneath the Stars of the Ancients, who grew from the ashes of the Dark Times to overcome the enemies of The First.

There was a lot more of the same; countless images flashed through my mind and the soft voice accompanied them, telling me the history of this being, this Keeper of the Sun Heart.

"So nothing shorter, then?" I said when the images stopped. "I think I'll call you The Keeper."

The Keeper was silent for a while. I tried to sit up again.

You need to lie for longer. You can talk. You can ask more questions.

More questions? Where would I start?

"Can't you read my mind? It seemed easy enough for your friend."

That is not my way. It is only the way of ...

There were the images of emptiness and oblivion again that I knew meant the black cloud that had been in my head.

The images still drew me down into a place of absolute darkness. To balance these thoughts, I brought to mind a film I had seen a few years ago that had made me laugh at how humanity always seemed to fail to overcome its more destructive tendencies. The film was called Dark Star. I thought that would be a good name for the other being. A name that would allow me not to get consumed by the associated images.

Dark Star, said The Keeper. *That is a good name.*

"So you do read my mind?"

Some things are so clear they stand out and I need only brush your mind with mine. But your mind is mostly confused and it would be better for you to speak your thoughts.

"What are you? Are you alive? I mean, are you a machine?"

At one time we had bodies that could move themselves. We can no longer do that. We have moved beyond physical necessities. Inside this shell there is a body, which at one point was not that different from your own.

An arm-like section of the shell separated from the main cylinder and was held out, as if in greeting. The surface at the end retreated, revealing something that resembled a slim flipper.

This is what my body looks like now.

I stared at the form that was extended towards me. It looked frail and somehow unfinished; like the drawing of a child. These people had built spaceships and travelled between the stars, but this hand couldn't hold a pen or even open a door.

Did they once have fingers that could design and build and create art?

You may touch if you wish.

The end of the platform rose up behind my head and shoulders so that I was lying up, as if resting against pillows. I raised my own arm and reached out slowly to touch the outstretched hand.

I hesitated, and my thoughts must have been clear to The Keeper.

The shell protects me. You cannot harm me. Neither can I harm you.

I let the ends of my fingers connect with the smooth surface at the end of the hand. I wasn't sure what to expect, but I suppose it was a relief to feel something akin to my own hand.

The Keeper was showing me that it was just like me. That it was made of flesh and bone, or at least something equally fragile and flawed.

"Where do you come from?" I asked.

My people are The First.

"The First? The First what?" I asked.

We are the first people in the galaxy, the first life to build civilisations and travel to the stars. We have searched everywhere, but have not found any other people as old as ourselves. We gave ourselves a different name in ages past, but have been called The First by all other people for so long *that we have forgotten what we were called.**

"You have forgotten the name of your people?"

We have forgotten a great number of things in our time. Our sun burned out before your world had formed. In that time we have created and destroyed countless civilisations.

"How old are you?"

In your timescale I am over a million years old.

My mind tried to grasp the sheer enormity of that time and what it might mean to be alive for so long.

The Keeper must have sensed my inability to understand the scale of such a life.

A lot of that time was spent sleeping.

I laughed. "Well, I'm glad you have a sense of humour at least."

I did not intend to be humorous, but it is good to hear you laugh. I am sure that there was a time when my people also laughed, but if there was, we have forgotten how to do that as well now.

"So what do you do now? Why are you here?" I asked, a note of concern entering my voice.

There is no need to be alarmed. It is a long time since we have interfered with another planet or civilisation. We have learnt to leave things as we find them.

"Really? What about the bears and the fox? They seem to be trapped here and I don't think their singing or powers of communication came naturally."

It is true that I have altered these animals. They have been with me for over a thousand years.

"A thousand years?" I was struggling to take all this in. "But how... why?"

I find them useful in making the first contact with the few people who venture into the bay. When I leave, the bears and the fox will be exactly as they were.

"Okay, but what about the impossible snow? What happens to that when you leave?"

The snow is my ship and will leave with me.

"Your ship?"

Yes.

I remembered trying to dig into the snow with my shovel and how I couldn't touch it or affect it in any way.

"Your ship is made of snow?"

Apart from what you see around you, my ship is made of snow at the moment. It will reform to become a ship capable of travelling between the stars when I leave.

"Just like that?" I wasn't sure how well sarcasm translated into dream-speak, but The Keeper seemed to understand.

The ship has its own power source, but it is limited. I cannot reform or move the ship without the Sun Heart.

"But you are The Keeper of the Sun Heart, aren't you?" I asked, puzzled.

The Keeper was silent and I felt nervous as I realised what this might mean.

"Wind Over Mountain said that you lost 'The Light'," I continued cautiously. "Is that what he calls the Sun Heart?"

Yes.

"He said it was stolen."

This is true.

"You've mentioned the Sun Heart to me in images," I said. "But you've never shown me what it actually looks like."

That is because it would not mean anything to you unless you had already seen it.

There was another uncomfortable silence.

This is what the Sun Heart looks like when it is closed and inactive.

The Keeper showed me an image of the small grey ball I had taken from my father.

I believe you have seen this before.

So, The Keeper had read my mind and knew that I had found my father; knew that I had taken the Sun Heart from him and knew that I had sent it back.

"You read my mind again then?" I accused The Keeper.

It was impossible to sense any emotional state from the featureless white of The Keeper's outer covering, but there was a pause in the images, which felt like a sigh.

I am trying to understand the events that have taken place just as much as you. Dark Star will have read your mind the first time you came to the bay. But Dark Star did not attack then. The only possible reason for Dark Star to attack you when

110

you returned a second time was if you had gained knowledge of the Sun Heart. I read your mind only enough to confirm this and discover what had taken place.

"What makes the Sun Heart so special?" I asked. "It seems quite small for something that can power your ship."

It is far more powerful than that. It has almost limitless power. It is the heart of a dying star.

"A star?"

Yes.

"A real star?"

Yes.

"You're saying that inside the object I took from my father there is an actual star?"

Yes.

"A star like our sun, which weighs hundreds of thousands of times more than the Earth and has a gravitational pull strong enough to hold the planets in motion?"

Yes, although the star that is in this Sun Heart was a hundred times larger than your sun when it was active.

"But that's impossible."

We are capable of many things that you would think impossible.

"How is it possible?"

This is not something that I fully understand. I do know that a large percentage of the energy of a Sun Heart is used in dispersing the gravity field, so that objects are unaffected by the presence of a Sun Heart.*

"And how does it do that?"

The First learnt how to manipulate matter long ago. It was the creation of the Sun Hearts that gave this knowledge an almost infinite power source.

"You can manipulate matter?"

This is how I can turn a spaceship into snow, or read your mind.

"My mind and snow are very different things," I observed.

Are they?

"My thoughts and memories aren't physical objects."

I have no doubt that Dark Star was able to look through your memories. And you have seen that I can read your thoughts. How can we do this if they are not physical?

"Yes, but…" I was lost in a world of the impossible.

These things are hard for you to understand. Your people have only just discovered the forces that bind everything together or hold them apart. We have known how to alter these forces for hundreds of millions of years.

"But how do you even get inside my head?" I reasoned. "Or inside an atom to do all these things?"

There was a pause that seemed like another sigh. I started to feel like a child asking its parents questions when they knew I wouldn't understand the answers.

*The very forces that hold matter together or keep it apart generate waves. These waves are the smallest things in the *universe, but they are everywhere and their existence creates paths that join everything together. We can control these paths and use them to change the forces that bind objects together. The space between atoms, the space between you and me, between myself and the mountains, between this world and your moon, are all equally accessible to us. We can move planets inside solar systems as easily as we can move particles inside atoms. We can reshape space and matter.*

"That's a lot to take in."

It is. But it is important that you understand the nature of the object your father took.

"If it's so powerful," I asked, "How did my father manage to take it from you in the first place?"

It was not expected.

"Not expected?"

No. Your father taking the Sun Heart would be like you leaving a dog in a car and coming back to find it had driven the car away.

"Are you saying we are like dogs to you?"

You are like dogs in that I do not expect you to be able to control the Sun Heart any more than you expect a dog to be able to control a car.

"So now you want me to return it to you?"

Yes.

I didn't say anything else for a while.

"How can I understand you now?" I asked eventually, as

113

a means of not talking about what was going to happen to me if I actually managed to return with the Sun Heart. "If it's the power of the Sun Heart that allows me to talk to you and the bears and the fox, how is this happening now?"

The ship also provides this function, but its power is limited and does not extend beyond the boundaries of the ship.

"Is that why I could only understand Wind Over Mountain and the fox when I was standing in the snow field?"

Yes, it is the contact with the ship that enables you to interpret their song.

"The way I understand you feels different, though; clearer."

It is not the ship that allows you to understand me now.

"What do you mean, now?"

There was another pause, but this didn't feel like a sigh.

Your body ceased to function and was badly damaged.

"Ceased to function?" I asked. "You mean I died?"

Yes.

Chapter 13

Modifications

"How long was I in the water?" I asked, trying to stay calm.

You were not in the water long before Wind Over Mountain brought you out. But it was enough to stop your body from functioning. Your body was damaged more by Dark Star.

"Dark Star attacked me?"

Yes.

"When I was already dead?"

That is what happened.

"Why would Dark Star do that?"

You expelled Dark Star from your mind. Dark Star thought this was not possible for you to do by yourself and that it was the Sun Heart that enabled you to do this.

"I suppose in a way it did. It was thinking about the Sun Heart that allowed me to drive Dark Star out of my head."

Dark Star would have seen this. Since the Sun Heart was not among your possessions, Dark Star believed you must have it hidden inside your body.

"Inside my body?"

Yes. Dark Star has not studied your people as have I.

"So what did Dark Star do?"

Dark Star looked inside your body.

I looked at my body.

"Your people are able to see through objects?"

No, we cannot do this.

"But you have scanners, or things that can do this?"

The Sun Heart is special and cannot be detected by anything other than the senses.

"So how did Dark Star look inside my body?"

Dark Star removed your head and cut your body into two pieces.

"What?" I checked over my body again and felt all around my neck, but there was nothing. "There are no marks," I said, hesitant with disbelief. I suddenly remembered my hands and put them in front of me to look at them. I turned them over and back again to examine them more closely.

"My fingers are back." I was aware my voice was shaking.

It is hard for you to imagine the things that we are able to do. If my ship can turn into snow and reform into a ship capable of travelling through space, you must realise that it is a simple thing to rebuild your body.

"That doesn't make it any easier to accept.' I fell silent again for a bit.

"Couldn't you have stopped Dark Star? You stopped the attack on Wind Over Mountain and the fox."

I see many things. I did not see this.

Neither of us spoke. After a while, The Keeper said, *you find drinking tea relaxing. Would you like some tea now?*

It sounded so strange and also so normal. A being from

another planet was asking me if I wanted a cup of tea.

"Why don't I feel hungry or thirsty? I can't have eaten or drunk anything for hours – days, even."

You are fully nourished. You do not require food or drink. I offer you tea because it helps you to relax.

A small section of the wall near me receded, leaving a hole. Inside was a cup, steaming and giving off the unmistakable smell of freshly poured tea. The cup was from a set I remembered from my childhood that my mother only used when we had visitors.

I picked up the tea and sipped out of the impossible cup that had been recreated perfectly from my mind. The tea was hot and soothing and it did relax me.

"So I've been brought back from the dead and rebuilt after I had been cut up into pieces?"

Yes. You have also been modified.

"Modified?"

I sat bolt upright and the tea spilt over my chest.

Yes.

I looked at the tea running down my chest. It should have scalded me, but although I could feel that it was hot there was no sensation of burning. The tea vanished, but looking in my cup I saw that it was full again.

"I thought you didn't interfere with anything."

It was necessary.

"How have I been modified?"

You are more efficient than you were.

"Efficient? In what way?"

As you have witnessed, your body can withstand heat. It can also withstand cold. You would be able to stand outside without protective clothing for any length of time and be unaffected by the temperature. Your skin can also not easily be damaged by objects.

"You mean that I'm indestructible?"

There are limits to what you can withstand.

"So, no jumping into volcanoes?"

That would not be wise.

I put the teacup down.

"May I have my clothes now?"

A section of the wall at the end of the platform came out like a drawer and I could see my clothing and other items inside.

I got up and started dressing.

"How long does this new, more efficient body last? Will I still grow old?"

You will not age. I have provided you with some of the last power from my ship. This is what renews you and keeps you alive. It might last a hundred years, it might last a thousand years, I do not know. It depends on how much you use the power to do anything other than keep you alive.

"I'm not sure that I understand. What else would I do?"

You will learn in time everything that you can now do.

I was putting my shirt on, relishing the fact that I could

do the buttons up again without the fumbling of my damaged fingers.

"You could have kept me exactly as I was though, couldn't you?"

Yes, I could have done this.

"So, why didn't you?"

You must retrieve the Sun Heart and return it to me. Dark Star will do everything possible to take the Sun Heart from you when you return. You would not succeed without the modifications.

"And why does Dark Star want the Sun Heart?"

Dark Star wishes to use the Sun Heart to destroy your planet.

Chapter 14

The Keeper's Dilemma

I sat down on the platform to steady myself.

"Sorry? Destroy the planet? Why would Dark Star want to do that?"

That is not easy to explain.

I waited for the explanation, but it didn't come.

"And exactly how would Dark Star use the Sun Heart to destroy the planet?" I asked.

With the power of the Sun Heart, Dark Star could pull the Moon into the Earth, remove the oceans and the seas and turn your entire world into a desert. There is nothing Dark Star would not be able to do once in possession of the Sun Heart.

"Why can't you stop Dark Star? You have power, even without the Sun Heart."

It is difficult for you to understand. We cannot end each other's life and that is the only thing that will stop Dark Star.

"You can't kill each other, but you can destroy our planet and everything on it?"

Yes.

"That is difficult to understand."

We do not have choices in the way that you understand them. We have laws built into us when we are created.

"You were 'created'?"

Yes, as were you.

"But that is not what you meant."

No. I was not created by a purely natural process. We are biological beings, but we are designed and created to perform specific roles. Your race is not very far from being able to do the same. It is how species survive beyond their natural limitations. I was created to be The Keeper of a Sun Heart, to protect our people.

"Protect?"

Yes.

"From what I've seen, you were created as a weapon, to use the Sun Heart to destroy other civilisations so that your people could colonise and survive."

What you have seen is only part of our history. At first the Keepers were created as weapons and they and the Sun Hearts enabled our people to expand and rule vast areas of the galaxy for millions of years. But I was created for a different purpose, as we started to lose control of our systems.

"How could you ever lose control if the Sun Hearts are as powerful as you suggest?"

As the Sun Hearts were used up or destroyed we became less able to defend ourselves. We also changed. We lost the desire to expand, to control.

"How do I know that what you're telling me is true? That if I return with the Sun Heart you will not try to take over this planet for your people?"

You can see what is in my mind. The sounds I make are automatic translations of the images in my mind. I cannot change or control these. The images in my mind are my experiences and my thoughts on my experiences. You see exactly what I have seen.

"I'm sure you can hide whatever you don't want me to see."

I can do this, but I cannot show you anything that is not true. I have told you what I am and it cannot be other than this.

"Do you not imagine things differently than how they are? Do you not dream?"

We do not dream.

"But how can you have made everything you have? How could you have created the Sun Heart and built ships that can turn into snow and travel to the stars without imagining these things?"

We see only what is possible, not what is impossible.

"Some people might say that is better than dreaming."

We do not know how to do otherwise. Our planet shone with the light of a thousand suns. We evolved with no sight. Our world is described in sound, our darkness is silence. But for us, sounds only describe what is real. We cannot create music and art. We do not invent stories and dances. Our worlds had countless sounds, but did not have any of these things.

That is why I am here.

"Really? Why?"

Of all the inhabited planets that I have visited, there are none that produce sounds in the variety and complexity that is found here. As you have not visited any other planets, you cannot know this.

I heard some music I recognised. A Mozart symphony, but somehow different. The instruments sounded broader and there were other sounds, almost like birdsong, playing along with the melody.

"It sounds very different to how I remember it."

You have not heard this. This is what the composer was thinking as the music was created.

The full implications of what The Keeper had said slowly dawned on me.

"Are you saying that I'm listening to Mozart's mind?"

Yes.

I listened for a while longer, unable to believe what I was hearing. These sounds somehow linked me to a man who had died hundreds of years ago. Passages of music kept repeating and I wondered if this was when they were actually being written down for the first time; that I was experiencing, moment for moment, what Mozart had experienced as he sat at his desk, trying to put these sounds down on paper, somehow translating all of this musical complexity into small dots and marks. The music went back a section and changed slightly as a passage was re-worked. Then it continued without stopping, a moment of creation unfurling effortlessly inside this extraordinary mind.

I began to feel that I was intruding; peeping in uninvited to a most private place.

"So you got inside his head and took what you wanted? I thought that was not your way."

The mind of this composer was not normal. It was greatly unsettled, but amid the chaos, the music stood out with a clarity that enabled me to take everything directly from his mind without any interference. There are very few people with whom I am able to do this.

"How do you normally record the sounds? I don't imagine that you stand around concerts with a microphone and a tape recorder?"

In effect, this is what I did. The Sun Heart allowed me to listen to any sound anywhere on the planet. People playing or singing, the rhythm of dances, birdsong, or the calls of the animals. Each sound I would store and send to my people.

The music stopped abruptly.

"And what do they do with them?"

You cannot imagine the effect that such sounds have on the senses of my people. A people who live in a world of sound, but who are unable to create a sound that does not have a purpose, unable to invent, unable to imagine anything past what is possible, unable to dream. We are transported by such sounds, to experience sensations and feelings that would otherwise be completely unattainable.*

"How long have you been collecting all these sounds from our planet?"

I have been here for around ten thousand years.

"Ten thousand years? Haven't you collected enough yet?"

We have a very different perspective on time. A thousand years is not a long time for us, and your world changes so quickly. It will not be long before there is no more birdsong and you yourselves will have forgotten how to sing. We have seen this many times. Like us and other species before you, you will eventually make your world uninhabitable.

"If you think that we are going to destroy our world anyway, why does Dark Star want to do this now?"

It is not just your world. There are thousands of worlds like this, where we listen to the rhythms and dances of life. Dark Star would destroy them all.

I stood up and paced back and forth, trying to imagine that I was asleep or unconscious. But all I could feel was the strength and life in my body, the whiteness of my surroundings and the silence of The Keeper waiting for me to say something.

"Why would Dark Star do this?"

Dark Star believes that the purpose of life is to have an end, that our life no longer has any meaning and that our end is long overdue. If all those worlds were destroyed, our lives would end as well. Dark Star knows this.

"Are you saying that these planets are keeping you alive?"

We are in the final stages of our life as a species. Our physical bodies have reached the limit of any changes that can be made to them. We have lost the will to conquer and control and we now exist merely as wanderers who live only through the experiences of others. Your world and others like it give us a reason to live, to go on breathing.

Suddenly I felt the countless ages in The Keeper's voice. The immeasurable years of existence and the weight of time bearing down, squeezing and pulling, until life became no more than gossamer strands stretched too tightly over the endless experiences.

"Why don't you give up? Why do you want to carry on?" I asked.

Why does any life want to carry on? Our survival is also built into us. We can no more end ourselves than we can end each other. But what you have just seen in me now is also what would enable Dark Star to eventually possess the Sun Heart again.

"Again?"

Dark Star is from the old times and was the previous Keeper of this Sun Heart. But Dark Star committed a crime against our race. I was created and the Sun Heart was given to me.

"And now Dark Star wants it back to destroy our world?"

That would be the first act of Dark Star.

"But you're over a million years old. How has it taken Dark Star this long to find you?"

Dark Star has found me many times. Each time, we have fought. Each time, I have disabled the ship of Dark Star and left for another planet. Each time, the ship of Dark Star has been rebuilt and each time Dark Star has found me again.

"Couldn't you just destroy the ship to stop Dark Star finding you?"

I am unable to do this, as this would result in the end of Dark Star.

"So the two of you have been chasing each other across the galaxy for hundreds of thousands of years?"

Yes.

"But this time it's different. You lost the Sun Heart."

Indeed. This time it is different.

Something still didn't make sense.

"How long has Dark Star been here?"

Dark Star has only just arrived on this world.

"When I first came here I saw a star fly overhead and then a great storm appeared from nowhere that raged for hours."

That was the arrival of Dark Star. Our fight lasted much longer than normal, as I did not have the Sun Heart. Dark Star was trying to make me reveal where the Sun Heart was. I did not want to lose all the power from my ship and in the end I revealed that I no longer had the Sun Heart and that I did not know where it was.

"But it was just on the other side of those mountains," I said, pointing in frustration at a random part of the chamber.

Yes, that is where your father took the ship, but I had no knowledge of where the ship ended. It could have flown anywhere on your planet and I would not have known where it was.

I lowered my arm slowly. Although I had always wondered how the ship ended up on a mountain, I had never imagined my father was responsible. Did all this happen like it had in my dream? I tried to remember what he had been doing in my dream.

"It was my father who flew the ship over the mountain?"

Yes.

"But how?"

The only way the ship could have flown over the mountains would be by using the Sun Heart.

"But that would mean my father could control the Sun Heart."

That would be the only possible conclusion.

"How could he do this?"

This is also something that I do not understand. The Sun Heart is intended to respond only to me. It has been tuned to life on this planet in order that I can understand the life here and communicate with it. People and animals vary in the levels to which they are tuned to the Sun Heart. It is possible that your father, and yourself, are highly harmonised with the Sun

*Heart.**

"So, my father takes the Sun Heart from you, somehow learns how to use it and flies the ship over a mountain, where it crashes. Does any of this sound possible to you?"

It is highly improbable, but I do not see any other alternative.

"Couldn't you have stopped him? Couldn't you have followed him over the mountain?"

My ship cannot move without the Sun Heart and I cannot move far from the ship, or for long. The power to control objects comes from our ships or the Sun Hearts. Our shells have power only to keep us alive.

"But you can control things outside the snow field from here."

I can do this, but I was unable to stop the ship from passing over the mountains.

"And Dark Star? Why didn't Dark Star go and look for it?"

Our first battle drained most of the power from our ships. Neither Dark Star nor myself can move from here without the Sun Heart.

"So, if I hadn't turned up, both of you would just be sitting here now, waiting for all eternity?"

That is correct.

"But I still don't understand. If I bring the Sun Heart back, Dark Star will take it from me. If I manage to give it back to you, you will leave and Dark Star will keep finding you until you lose possession of the Sun Heart and then one day our world will explode."

What you say is true. But losing the Sun Heart has created a different possibility.

"Which is?"

I have predicted that at some point Dark Star will overcome our inbuilt laws and will end my life to regain possession of the Sun Heart.

"How would Dark Star do this if you have the Sun Heart to defend yourself?"

I cannot defend against everything that Dark Star is capable of doing at all times. I also cannot match the desire of Dark Star. Eventually Dark Star would succeed. Maybe even this time. I cannot tell.

"So, how does losing the Sun Heart help here?"

If your father was able to control the Sun Heart, there is a high probability that you can also control it.

I started to feel uneasy about what The Keeper was expecting me to do.

"You mean if I learn to control the Sun Heart I will be able to defend myself against Dark Star?"

Yes.

"But you don't just want me to be able to defend myself, do you?"

There was no response to this question.

"You want me to stop Dark Star altogether? You want me to end the life of Dark Star?"

I would not be able to countenance such an act. You must decide for yourself what the best course of action is for you and for your world.

I took that as a yes.

"How do I learn to control the Sun Heart?"

I will show you.

Part 3: The Crystal World
Chapter 15
Into the Sunheart

Uncle Digit stopped pushing me and looked around.

"Where are we?" he asked.

We were in a field that curved gently round to the left, following the course of the river. We had left the towpath and the town some while back.

"I don't know. We've never come this far before," I said.

"I think I'd better get you back to your mum before she starts wondering where we are."

"Aren't you tired from pushing me?" I asked him as he turned me round.

"Tired? I was just going to tell you what it was like travelling back with the changes The Keeper made to me."

The changes? I'd forgotten about them.

"Can you fly?" I asked excitedly.

"No, I can't fly," Uncle Digit said, laughing. "But it took me less than a day to get back to the skidoo instead of the normal two and a half."

"That sounds fast," I said.

"It was fast. It didn't matter how hard I ran, I never got out of breath or felt tired or cold. It was like I had my own jet pack that pushed me forwards and I just had to keep moving my legs to keep up with it."

"So you ran all the way over the mountains without stopping?"

"Pretty much. I can pull myself up rocks as if I weighed next to nothing, dig my fingers into ice and jump about ten feet straight up in the air. Once I got the hang of all this, I moved over the steeper sections of the route almost as quickly as I could run."

"Is there anything else you can do that you couldn't before?"

"Well, I haven't tried everything, but I can see in the dark now."

"Really?"

"Yes. Even when the wind and the snow reduces the visibility to almost nothing, I can clearly see everything gleaming with a silvery luminescence, like moonlight shining on water. There's no colour, but every detail stands out as if I were looking at an enlarged photograph. I wondered if it's how The First see things, using some form of echolocation."

"Like bats?"

"That sort of thing, yes."

It began to rain quite heavily and there was water running down my face.

"We need to get you home, Finn. Your mother's going to kill me."

"Maybe you need to use some of your special powers,

Uncle Digit," I said with a cheeky chuckle.

He laughed and started walking more quickly over the footpath. When we got back to the towpath he began to run, picking up speed until we were going so fast that I swear my wheelchair wasn't touching the ground. I was shrieking with the thrill of the speed and we were both laughing as we rocketed along. We went round a corner and just managed to avoid running over a man walking with his dog. We wished him 'good day' as we sped past, but calmed down and carried on slightly more carefully until we arrived home.

Mum must have been looking out for us, as the door opened before we got to it. She took one look at my sopping hair and clothes and gave a little groan.

"Henry, how could you?" she said.

"Sorry, sis, we went further than I meant to," said Uncle Digit.

Mum was clearly unimpressed. "Inside now and get out of those wet things."

We tried to look sheepish, but it was difficult not to keep smiling.

"I'm sorry, Mum, we just had such a good time."

"I'm sure you did, but I really don't want you catching a cold."

"Okay," I said, and Uncle Digit carried me upstairs quickly so that I could change.

After lunch, Uncle Digit and I went back up to my room

and sat at my table. I had so many questions I wanted to ask, but didn't know where to start. The joy of the morning was subsiding and I was coming to terms with the fact that Uncle Digit would be leaving again soon.

"I won't ever forget this holiday," I said.

"It hasn't finished yet," said Uncle Digit with a smile. "There's something else I wanted to show you."

"There's more?" I said eagerly.

"Oh yes. I hope so."

Uncle Digit had taken the Sun Heart from his coat pocket downstairs and he held it up to me.

"The Keeper showed me how to open this and how to use it."

"You're going to use it? Here?" My voice was unsteady.

"Just a little. If I can, there's something in here that might interest you."

"What is it?"

Uncle Digit put the Sun Heart between us on the table and looked at me.

"The Sun Heart is not just an amazing tool for making impossible things happen; it also records everything that happens to it. The Keeper told me that it would have not just recorded everything that happened when my father took the Sun Heart, but that it would have recorded all of his memories."

"But I don't understand. How could it do that?"

"I've no idea, but if it's true it means that my father's life is in here somewhere. If we can find his memories, we can see everything that happened to your grandfather when he left home and went on his voyage. We can see him meet The Keeper and take the Sun Heart. We can see everything as he experienced it. We can find out how his ship ended up halfway up a mountain."

"Do you know where your father's memories are? If they're inside the Sun Heart, how do you get them out?"

"Well, that's what I've got to find out. The Keeper showed me how to open the Sun Heart and told me that using it is a matter of how well I'm tuned to it, that I must let the Sun Heart guide me and that I have to learn how to influence it."

He picked up the Sun Heart and held it in front of his face.

"Right then. Here goes."

He closed his eyes and I could see him relax. Nothing happened for a minute or two and Uncle Digit remained motionless the whole time with his eyes closed.

He opened his eyes.

"Have you done it?" I whispered.

"I think so," he replied.

We were staring intently at the Sun Heart, looking for anything that was different. We looked at each other, but neither of us wanted to break the silence so we looked back at the ball.

At first there was nothing. Then, slowly, the surface started to dissolve. Just like Uncle Digit had described before, the ball began to give out light, which got brighter and brighter until we couldn't see each other. It wasn't a light that blinded you and made you flinch or look away, it just filled everything until there was nothing else but the light. Then, suddenly, the light was gone and we could see the ball in between us, glowing softly.

Uncle Digit removed his hands and the ball stayed where it was, hovering in the air.

"Gosh, are you controlling it?"

"No, I just opened it. This is what it does, I think."

"So, the Sun Heart's 'open' now?" I asked, bemused.

"Yes. It's activated and we're connected."

"Connected?" I queried. "What does that mean?"

"It feels like we can read each other's minds, if that makes any sense."

"Is it reading your mind now?"

"No, it's just waiting."

Uncle Digit started moving his head around.

"What's up?" I asked.

"It's strange," he said. "Even though it's right in front of me, it's not in the way. It's like I can see it and see through it at the same time."

Uncle Digit got up and walked about the room. The glowing ball moved with him, staying the same distance from him all the time.

"It must stay in the position I leave it until I touch it again."

"What happens then?"

Uncle Digit reached up and touched the ball. The glow vanished and the ball thudded softly to the floor and stayed there, a simple, smooth grey ball again.

We both looked at it.

"It shuts down?" I suggested.

"It certainly looks that way."

Uncle Digit bent down and picked up the Sun Heart. He sat back down and held the ball in his hands as before.

"Let's see if we can find anything, shall we?"

He closed his eyes again and opened them almost straight away.

"Did you..." I began, but the ball burst into light before I could finish. The light retreated and Uncle Digit took his hands away, leaving the glowing Sun Heart between us.

"That was quick," I said, looking up at Uncle Digit.

"It was, wasn't it?" He didn't take his eyes from the ball and was staring at it with a slightly quizzical expression.

"Didn't you expect it to do that?"

"Not really. It's like it knows me now. I can feel it reaching out to me, inviting me in."

"Do you know how to get inside it?" I asked.

He looked up at me. "Yes, I think I do."

Uncle Digit looked at the Sun Heart again and didn't say anything for a few moments.

Then he looked up in surprise. He looked at me and around

the room and seemed to be disorientated.

"Gosh, I'm sorry. I didn't intend to be gone for so long."

"What do you mean?" I asked. "You just said that you thought you knew how to get inside the Sun Heart and I was waiting to see what would happen next."

"But I feel like I've been gone for hours."

"It was just a few seconds ago."

Uncle Digit nodded as if accepting this himself.

"Okay," he said. "Let me try again. Can you time me?"

He looked back at the Sun Heart and I watched his face carefully. He blinked a few times, then his face froze. I looked at my watch and made a note of the time.

Thirty seconds later, he was back.

"How long was it that time?" he asked.

I told him and he looked shocked.

"Really? Okay. Let's try for a bit longer this time."

And he was gone again. I looked at my watch and watched the seconds go by.

I wanted to reach out and touch his hand to see what would happen, but I was afraid that it would bring him back before he'd finished, so I stayed still, studying his face, waiting for him to blink again.

After a few minutes I started to get worried and wondered if I should try and bring him back anyway. I was reaching out to touch his hand when he sat back and let out a huge breath as if he'd been under water all this time.

He stared at me and looked like he was trying to remember where he was.

"Right," he said at last. "How long was I gone for that time?"

I looked at my watch. "Just over three minutes. How long did it feel like you had been gone for?"

"A long time. Weeks, months. Time doesn't have the same meaning in there."

"What's it like?" I asked, trying to stay calm.

Uncle Digit's eyes were shining with mischief. "Do you want to see for yourself?" he asked.

I couldn't work out if he was being serious or not. "Do you mean I can do it as well?"

He didn't saying anything, but his smile broadened.

"Really?"

Uncle Digit stopped smiling. "I'm pretty sure we can do it, yes. But it's not easy. I can help, but you will need to learn to do some things for yourself."

"But how did you find out how to do all this so quickly?"

"Remember, I've spent a long time in there," he said, nodding at the Sun Heart. "The Keeper gave me some guidance, but most of it I learned just now. Some things seemed to come naturally though, as if I had done them before. Maybe this is what The Keeper meant by being 'in tune' with the Sun Heart. Your grandfather was certainly in tune with it, judging from what I've seen."

"You saw your father?" I asked.

"Yes, in one sense I did."

"Will I get to see him as well?"

"Yes – that's one of the main things I want you to see."

"What do you mean 'in one sense'?"

"What you will see are all his memories and experiences that have been stored in the Sun Heart. It's like watching a film except you're seeing everything from his perspective, as if he's holding the camera."

"Okay."

"But, you will also know what he was feeling a lot of the time, and some of that can be difficult. Do you want to try?"

"Yes, please," I said.

Uncle Digit closed his eyes and didn't say anything for a few moments. Then, without opening his eyes, he said, "Can you feel anything different?"

I had thought it was getting warmer and that the air was moving around, as if the window was open on a warm summer's day.

"It feels like there is a slight breeze in here. It's like something soft is brushing against my face."

"That's the Sun Heart's way of saying 'hello'. Now close your eyes and concentrate on the breeze brushing your face."

I closed my eyes. "Okay," I said.

"Now, imagine the table and me sitting opposite you, exactly as if your eyes were open."

This wasn't as easy as it sounded, but I managed a kind of blurry representation of the table and a figure opposite.

"Okay. It's not very clear," I said.

"Don't worry, it should be getting clearer now. This is the part that I can control."

As if someone were wiping the dirt from a window, the image in my head became clearer and clearer until it was hard to imagine that I wasn't sitting there with my eyes open.

"You look real," I said in shock. "Like you're actually there. I can see every detail in your face."

I opened my eyes and looked at the real Uncle Digit. Then I closed them again. He was still there, exactly the same, except in my head his eyes were open and there was no Sun Heart between us.

Open your eyes again.

I opened my eyes.

You can now see and hear me in your mind.

I had distinctly heard Uncle Digit's voice, but his mouth hadn't moved.

"How are you doing that?" I asked.

You try. Stop speaking and just think what you want to say, like you're talking to yourself.

"Okay," I said.

This can't be working, I thought to myself.

Oh, but it is, I heard Uncle Digit reply in my head.

Wow, I don't believe this.

142

Then my thoughts got very jumbled up. I told myself to relax.

That's right, Uncle Digit said. *Just relax. Close your eyes again and imagine that you're talking to yourself. Those top thoughts are the ones that will come out.*

I closed my eyes again and concentrated on what I was seeing.

There's nothing behind you, just a soft light; it's like we're sitting in an endless desert, or the whole sky is inside the room with us.

This is what I call the Waiting Room. We're not inside the Sun Heart yet. That's what I'm going to do now. Ready?

Sure, I said, anything but sure.

I felt things starting to shift. Slowly at first and then much faster. The endless, flat surface gathering in, getting closer and closer, but somehow not changing. Everything became enormous and tiny at the same time, as if the world was turning inside out and the universe was being pulled over my head like a jumper.

Then I was sitting at my table again, looking at Uncle Digit smiling at me.

Chapter 16
Another World

I looked around me at a scene I knew couldn't have come from my imagination.

A clear night sky teemed with countless stars, saturating everything with speckled light and making it as bright as day. A huge misty-blue planet, with tilted rings like Saturn, dominated the panorama. Low down, a red and purple cloud shot through with bursts of orange and yellow fire hung on the horizon, sparkling above a large mountain range in the distance.

The surrounding mountains shone with colour. Huge crystal structures sprouted like coral from their steep sides. Great towering columns and branching fans of red, blue, green and gold glowed and glistened all over the slopes and valleys.

We were close to the base of one mountain with veins of amber-like pure orange, smooth as glass, ascending straight up for thousands of feet.

Where are we? I asked.

I think this is The Keeper's current home world. It looks like it's one of the moons of that planet, doesn't it? This is where I come every time I enter the Sun Heart.

Every time? How often have you done this? I thought you'd only been here once or twice.

I spent some time practising getting here and leaving to make sure I could always do it. I wasn't going to bring you here unless I knew we could get back easily.

What do you think that is? I asked, pointing at the large red and purple cloud.

I'm not sure. It might be a nebula. Do you know what that is?

No.

It's a mass of gas and dust, either the remnants of an exploded star or where new stars are being formed, or both, I suppose.

Gosh. I thought you could only see things like that with a telescope.

This world must be much closer to the centre of the galaxy than we are. There are countless more stars visible here than in our night sky.

Have you ever been here during the day?

There is no day here as we would know it.

So the sun never comes up?

I think that star is the sun for this system, Uncle Digit said, pointing up to the largest star in the sky.

I looked at the star, so far away. *It seems very small to be a sun.*

Yes. It must be really cold here. There's no life, no atmosphere, no wind, no sound at all, just the silence of space.

Why would they choose this for a home?

I think that they like it like this, completely silent. They don't want any distractions. This is where they listen to the sounds of the universe.

The sounds of the universe? I repeated, not quite sure what he meant.

Yes. This is where The Keeper and all the other Keepers on all the other worlds send the sounds they have collected.

What do they do with them?

That was one of the things I thought you would want to find out. But you might be interested in seeing this first.

Seeing what? I asked.

Uncle Digit pointed.

My bedroom table was in the middle of a dull, featureless grey road, about as wide as a tennis court. I looked to where Uncle Digit was pointing. Speeding towards us was what looked like an elegant chess piece, dressed in green and black robes. It must have been at least ten feet tall.

I looked back at Uncle Digit. He didn't seem concerned.

What is it? I asked.

That's one of The First, he replied calmly.

Really?

Yes.

You mean there is an alien coming towards us?

Yes.

Can it see us? I asked.

No, it can't see us or touch us.

We watched it come closer. It was headed straight for us. I looked at Uncle Digit to see what he would do, but he just sat there, looking at a being from another world coming towards us as if it were the most normal thing ever.

I looked back as it bore down on us. It looked so real, so solid. I tried to stay calm, telling myself that Uncle Digit knew what he was doing.

It was nearly on us and I instinctively tried to move my wheelchair out of the way, but the wheels wouldn't turn.

I waited for the crash, but it never came. The being floated straight through the table and us as if we weren't there and continued up to the base of the mountain.

Bit unnerving, isn't it? said Uncle Digit.

Just a bit, I said, trying to breathe normally again.

I've been here quite a few times now and that one always comes up just after I enter. It's like we're watching the same film from the beginning each time we come in.

What's it doing? I asked.

The being stopped a few feet from the mountain face. Some of the road surface rose up to cover the rock until it was just above the creature's head. The road turned from dull grey to transparent and through it the amber veins stood out even more intensely, with thousands of golden lights dancing against the pure orange.

I thought they were blind, I said. *How can they see all the different lights and colours?*

147

The crystals must be reflecting or emitting sounds that we can't hear. What you and I see through the road is the colours getting brighter. To them the material of the road must be enhancing something other than light. Whatever is happening, it seems to be quite addictive for them.

There are no sounds, though? I can't hear anything.

No, there is no atmosphere here, so we can't hear any sound.

But they hear things?

Yes, I believe so. What I do know is that this road and all the other roads and places I've seen have been formed from their spaceship. Just like the snow was from The Keeper's ship, only much bigger.

You mean we're sitting on a spaceship?

Kind of, yes. It can become whatever they want it to. It provides them with everything they need. When they want something, like that material there, it just appears out of the road. I think it also somehow provides a way for them to communicate and allows our friend there to be able to hear the sounds from the mountain.

Uncle Digit stood up. He looked down at me.

Do you want to see more?

Of course.

The Crystal World

Chapter 17
The Crystal Lake

I moved my hands up to the wheels of my chair and tried to move backwards again, but nothing happened.

My chair won't move.

You'll have to get used to controlling things here.

Can't you come round and push me?

No, it's not like that. What we're seeing are lots of images all cleverly linked together like a three-dimensional film. You can't move through the mages; you have to make the images move through you.

Can't you make them move for both of us?

I could, but you'll have a lot more fun if you learn to do this for yourself. You'll get the hang of it in the end.

It was tricky, learning to move everything past me instead of trying to move forward. I kept losing control of the flow of movement and could only proceed in fits and starts to begin with.

Slowly, my brain adapted to this new method of motion and I moved faster, without faltering.

We still weren't making much headway though.

Have we got far to go? I asked.

You'll start going faster in no time. And you don't have to stay on the road either, Dear Boy.

I looked down at Uncle Digit's feet. They weren't actually touching the ground. He rose off the ground a bit more, then started speeding up and was soon disappearing into the distance.

I laughed and tried to follow, but stayed where I was, moving slowly along the road.

I kept trying, though, and soon managed to control my surroundings so that I could move up as well as along, making my chair rise from the surface. I started to pull everything towards me more quickly, and began racing along, eventually overtaking Uncle Digit in a blur. He soon caught up with me again, flying along with his arms stretched out in front of him like Superman.

And there we were, the two of us, laughing and zooming along on a different world faster than a jet fighter.

I suddenly thought. *Do I need to keep my wheelchair?*

Do you think you can make yourself move along without it? Uncle Digit asked.

I think so. I suppose I just have to imagine that my wheelchair isn't here anymore.

Give it a go.

What if I fall?

I don't think you will, but you can't hurt yourself, even if you did fall.

Do you think I will able to walk here?

That would be something, wouldn't it, Champ? Can you

remember how to walk? You would have to be able to imagine yourself walking.

I'm not sure.

There's nothing wrong with trying. You'll have plenty of time to practise as we'll be here for a while yet.

Won't we have to get back soon?

Judging from my past visits, if we went back now it would be a few seconds after we left. We won't be here as long as I was the last time either.

I made my wheelchair disappear easily enough and I didn't fall to the ground, but it took me a while to work out how to change my position from sitting down to flying straight.

I imagined that I was lying on my front in bed and that seemed to work. I nearly screamed in delight as I started to fly along, as free as a bird, twisting and turning as the roads snaked through the mountain range.

In places the road was as wide as a motorway. In other places it was as narrow as a country track, always fitting seamlessly into the contours of the mountains through which we were travelling. I wondered when the mountains stopped.

Do you know where we're going? I asked Uncle Digit.

Yes, but we can go faster if you like.

We sped up and the mountains became more of a blur as we wound between them.

Do we have to follow the road? I asked.

No, we can go where we want, but the roads are useful

152

in guiding us. They go to and from points of interest. The one we are on goes from the Amber Mountain where we entered, to the Crystal Lake.*

The Crystal Lake? Is that where we're going?

It's one of the things I want to show you on the way.

Are we going to a city?

The First don't have cities as we know them. They don't have possessions, or houses, or offices, or factories. Everything they need is created for them by the ship.

I wanted to see more, so I stopped going forwards and shot upwards, climbing higher and higher, until I was above the mountains looking down across this world.

I stopped and floated there, suspended in space, looking at the expanse of mountains with all of the crystal colours sparkling in the constant starlight.

Uncle Digit joined me and looked down as well.

It's amazing, isn't it? he said.

I didn't say anything. I was just letting everything sink in. I could see more roads: dull veins of grey standing out against the dark rock and shining crystals.

Have you been on any of the other roads? I asked.

One or two. They all lead to different places of interest to The First. But nothing really compares to the Crystal Lake.

I followed the road we had been on with my eyes and saw that it disappeared around a very large mountain.

Is it on the other side of that mountain? I asked Uncle

Digit.

Yes, it is, he said.

Do we have to follow the roads? Can't we just fly to the mountain straight from here?

You don't even have to fly there if you don't want to.

How else would we get there?

I'll show you. Keep your eye on the mountain.

Then Uncle Digit disappeared. He just wasn't there anymore. I looked up at the mountain in the distance and saw something flashing at the top like a beacon. The flashing stopped and the next moment, Uncle Digit was standing by me again, smiling.

Did you see me shining at the top of the mountain? he asked.

Yes.

What do you think?

Can I do that?

I think so. Remember that we are inside the Sun Heart, that all of this is really just some very cleverly stored images and that you can control how you see them. It's not that different from moving away from the table, or being able to stand up in the sky like this.

How do I do it?

Let's go back down and you can start practising.

We flew down to the road and I practised zipping between objects, starting with ones close to me and moving myself further and further away, until we were both standing on the summit of the great mountain, looking down onto the Crystal Lake.

What is it? I asked.

Maybe it's the largest diamond in the galaxy.

Why do you call it a lake?

There's no liquid on this world, so there are no lakes as we know them. But to me it has the same feel as a beautiful expanse of water.

Neither of us spoke for a while. The giant crystal shone and sparkled, every colour imaginable reflecting and refracting over the millions of variations in the surface. Even moving slightly gave rise to large differences in what was being seen.

We flew slowly down the mountain. I could see that the road coming from the mountain went all the way around the lake. It didn't look grey like the one we had been on, but seemed to be composed of a pattern of undulating coloured dots.

What's that moving on the road around the lake? I asked Uncle Digit.

That is a lot more of The First.

Wow, I exclaimed. *For some reason I didn't expect there to be so many of them.*

I couldn't guess at the numbers that were moving around the vast crystal. There wasn't a part of the road that didn't have someone on it.

This race ruled the galaxy for millions of years. There

must still be billions of them left, scattered around different systems, slowly dying out on remote worlds such as this.*

You make it sound sad.

I suppose it is sad, he said, *But it's no different from how we live, really.*

Is this how we will end up? I asked.

Now there's a question! he replied with a laugh.

I looked at these beings, capable of doing anything, having anything, who chose to stare at crystals, listen to the sounds from other planets and walk around a diamond the size of a city.

Uncle Digit could sense what I was thinking.

These people have done everything, they have had everything. Now I suppose all they want is peace.

Soon we could make out individual bodies. Some of them were going around the lake one way and some were going the other way, each body moving in and out, opposing waves snaking through each other in a never-ending dance.

Why do you think they're moving like that? I asked.

I watched them for a long time on my first visit. I even went right down and walked with them, moving in the same way that they do. Although I got a better sense of the shifting colours when I was moving around, I felt there was more to what they were doing than just appreciating the light. There's something timeless and eternal about it, as if being here is a spiritual event.

Like going to church? I suggested.

I suppose you could look at it like that.

Do you think they believe in God?

I don't know what they believe, Dear Boy.

I watched them flowing round the lake, their never-ceasing movement seeming to me now like people at the destination of a great pilgrimage.

I had seen something similar last summer while we were on holiday in France. Mum mentioned that there was a town nearby where some people believed the water had been blessed by God and was sacred. They believed it could cure the incurable and might make someone well again who could not be helped by normal medicine.

"Do you believe that?" I asked her. I was surprised, as Mum never mentioned God. We didn't even go to church for Christmas. When I came back from school with questions about any religion, she would look blank, as if she was thinking about something completely different. Then she would ask me what I thought, listen to my answer and tell me that I was probably right.

But she looked at me carefully when I asked her if she believed in the powers of the water there and her mouth trembled slightly, as though she were on the edge of tears.

"I don't know what to believe anymore," she said. "But I want to make sure you have every chance there is to heal and to walk again, even if it might seem impossible."

I didn't say anything else, but I wasn't sure what to make of all this. Did I want to walk and run around like other children and did I get frustrated and angry because I couldn't do those simple things? Yes, of course I did. But I only knew life in my wheelchair and I didn't have any expectations of this ever changing. Could these sacred waters really make me walk again?

In the end it was agreed that we would go to the waters. We spent nearly the whole day in the town before going to the church to receive a blessing and then joining the queue of people waiting to take the water in the sacred grotto.

In the queue there were people in wheelchairs like myself. Some were being pushed along in hospital beds, still connected to tubes and bags. Almost everyone held prayer beads in their hands, slowly moving each bead through their fingers, their mouths quietly intoning words I could barely hear, and I became slightly hypnotised by the soft murmur of a hundred prayers rising up like the comforting sound of bees smothering lavender.

Was this what faith sounded like? I felt I didn't belong here in the midst of all this belief and hope.

In front of us, a young girl about my age walked slowly forward with her mother. She had a condition that left her body slightly twisted and she walked with a stoop, like a very little old lady.

Like me, the girl spent a good deal of time gazing around

her, looking at the people coming and going. But whereas I was getting nervous and felt as though I shouldn't really be there, she seemed calm and at ease. Whenever she caught my eye, she would smile at me and nod slowly in a knowing manner, as if she could somehow see and understand what was happening inside me and was agreeing with everything I thought.

At one point she leant forward, took my hand and said something to me in French that I didn't understand. Mum spoke very good French and I asked her what the girl had said. Mum paused and seemed uncertain. She was about to reply when the girl's mother explained in faltering English that her daughter had said Jesus would take away her pain and that she hoped he would set me free as well.

Mum looked surprised, but said in English, "thank you," adding, "we are also hoping for a miracle."

The girl's mother nodded stiffly before turning back and calling her daughter to do the same.

I didn't have time to ask anything further, as we had almost got to the front of the queue and were about to be separated. The girl went one way and I went the other, to be immersed in the extremely cold water, while prayers were said and water was put in bottles for us to take away.

As we left, I could see the girl ahead of us, leaving the area. She saw us and waved as she walked away, still hunched and still smiling. I waved goodbye to her and then she was gone.

I turned round to look at Mum as she pushed me.

"Why did you look surprised before, when the girl's mother spoke to us?"

"I don't know," Mum answered, "it just seemed odd."

"Odd? Why? Did the girl really say what her mother said? It didn't sound like what she said."

"Well, you must be doing very well in French at school," Mum said, laughing.

"It's just that I didn't hear the girl mention Jesus at all."

Mum stopped pushing me and bent down to kiss the top of my head.

"No, she didn't mention Jesus," she said. "I think that what the girl said upset her mother, which is why her mother told us something different."

"What did the girl say then?" I asked.

Mum sighed slightly. "She said that you mustn't worry. That it was just water and that whatever happens, God loves us for what we are."

She didn't say anything else and we continued on in silence.

And now, on a different world, watching The First moving around a place that seemed sacred to them, I wondered if the little girl was my fairy tale princess, like the one in Uncle Digit's story. Was she the defiant one? Was her defiance to smile and accept what she knew she couldn't change? And what was it that these ancient people, the last of The First, who had harnessed the power of the stars and had lived longer than anyone could imagine, what was it that they couldn't accept?

Uncle Digit woke me from my wonderings.

Penny for your thoughts, Dear Boy. You disappeared there for a bit and I couldn't follow you.

Sorry. It just reminded me of something. I wasn't sure that I could explain to Uncle Digit what I had been thinking about, so before my thoughts got too mixed up I quickly added, *Where are we going to next?*

We're going to find your grandfather's memories and see what happened to him.

Chapter 18
The Citadel

But how do we do that? I mean, we're flying around on a moon, inside the Sun Heart. How do we get to see what was inside my grandfather's head? Is there a special cinema here for viewing people's memories?

Uncle Digit laughed at that. *Actually, that's not a bad way of looking at it.*

Really?

Yes. My father's memories are stored in the same way as all the images we are looking at now. As we move around and jump from place to place, we're just accessing the images for whatever part we want to go to. This is quite easy, as we can see the path to the next image and move there.

But we can't see your father's memories.

No, we can't.

So how did you find where they are kept?

It took me a while, but in the end I let the Sun Heart guide me. I found that if I think about something, the Sun Heart helps to show me the way there. When I thought about my father and his journey, it took me to the Citadel.

The Citadel?

That's what I call it. The First probably have a much longer name for it, but basically it's a museum full of everything that they have ever collected from everywhere they have ever been.

     You mean like stuffed aliens and bits of old planets?

     You can joke now, but you wait until you see it. You would have to live as long as The First to see everything in there.

     Which way is it?

     Let's go back up.

We flew back up high above the Crystal Lake and hopped from mountain to mountain until the mountains ran out and the terrain became flatter. And there, stretched across the horizon, was the Citadel.

It was a smooth, featureless dome, entirely grey, like all of the roads leading to it. I couldn't imagine how big it was. From where we were it looked as though it could have been anywhere between ten and a hundred miles wide. All the roads leading from the mountains joined together into one wide road that led to the dome, and as we got closer we could see The First as they travelled to and from the Citadel.

We flew down to the road and followed a group going back. Uncle Digit and I chatted about the way they chose to look. We made up little stories about them, imagining them speaking to each other, asking each other about their day and what they had seen and done.

The wide road led to an opening about the size of the back of one of the enormous cargo ships that I used to watch coming and going from the port in town, but that was dwarfed by the scale of the building around it.

We followed the road through the opening and into the Citadel. Columns formed archways as tall and majestic as a cathedral nave that carried on for miles and disappeared into the centre of the Citadel far in the distance.

For the first time there was sound; lots of it. It was like thousands of people whistling different tunes. After the silence of outside, it seemed deafening.

What is it? I asked Uncle Digit.

That's The First talking to each other. There must be an atmosphere of some sort in here.

Can you understand what they are saying?

There's so much going on that it's hard. If I concentrate on one sound, I get some images in my mind, but they talk in ways and about things that make little sense to me.

We followed the columned road for a while, passing avenues that led away in all directions. These avenues were created from shapes and forms that bent and twisted, spiralling on top of each other, merging and separating, growing ever upwards and outwards and stretching further than we could see. The First travelled along them as if they were on a flat road, climbing and turning to follow the twisting of the structures as they headed wherever they were going.

It reminded me of a drawing I had seen where people walked up and down stairs in an elaborate structure. Everything looked perfectly normal from certain angles, but then you noticed that there were people walking upside down in relation to other people in the drawing, making everything suddenly look impossible.

We left the road and followed one of these avenues. At intervals on each side were large open areas containing objects.

I looked at Uncle Digit.

Here are your stuffed aliens and bits of old planets, he said.

The areas were situated in a way that separated them from everything else around them, giving the impression that they were unique spaces, somehow standing alone in their own world.

But things are moving. Is everything alive or are they images? I asked.

I've seen some of The First touch things, so I know they are real and not images. The Keeper told me that The First haven't interfered with any life form for millions of years, so these must be perfect copies, set in motion to display everything there is to know about the object.

There were entire buildings and edifices. There were beings from other worlds that moved or flew around. There were plants that swayed in breezes and some that moved by themselves as you watched. One large tree-like plant had a shining trunk and branches. The branches ended in metallic fan-like structures with hanging fruits that changed shape and colour continuously, making the whole tree breathe and evolve with each passing moment.

I could have stayed wandering along the avenues forever, but Uncle Digit reminded me why we were here, so we headed back to the road and on towards the centre of the Citadel.

As we got closer to the end of the road, the roof opened out more, revealing what at first looked like colourful, glittering fog. Then we emerged out into an open space shining with the brilliance of a billion lights. Among the lights were swirling and sparkling billows of purple, blue and red smoke rising up or stretching out like great storm clouds. In the centre was a giant ball of fire; the galaxy-sun around which all other objects revolved.

I gazed at it in wonder.

Do you know what it is? asked Uncle Digit.

It's amazing. Is it a galaxy? I asked.

Not just any galaxy. This is an exact copy of our galaxy. Every star, planet, moon, comet, black hole and gas cloud. Everything is here; moving, rotating, exploding and creating, just as it would be if you could travel out into space and see it all for yourself.

I was captivated by the sheer beauty and scale of the countless stars.

I couldn't take my eyes off it either when I first saw it, said Uncle Digit.

I carried on staring at it, losing myself in the patterns and swirls until I noticed something.

Some stars look different, I said. *I mean, they somehow don't look like stars.*

Yes, it's as though you're not quite sure how you're noticing them among all the other lights.

Something tells me you know what they are.

Uncle Digit pointed up into the luminous expanse of stars.

If you went up there into the galaxy to look at them more closely, you would see that they aren't stars at all.

What are they? I asked.

Each light shines where a world holds a Sun Heart.

All those are Sun Hearts? There were so many, it was impossible to count them all.

And there are thousands more you can't see from here.

And each one of them can show everything that is happening on that world?

Yes, they can.

I looked at the twinkling lights, shining among the surrounding stars, each one containing a Sun Heart, each one of them capable of showing a world of unknown skies and horizons, with unseen animals and plants, mountains and valleys, rivers and seas, cities, songs and dances.

I wish we could see them, I said, excited. *Can we connect to those Sun Hearts?*

No. Here inside this Sun Heart, they are all just images. All except one, of course, he added, mysteriously.

One? Which one?

Which one do you think?

The one we're in? The one for Earth?

Yes. If we find that one, we can do the same as all The First standing around here. We can listen to our planet and watch your grandfather's journey.

All The First? I had been so absorbed by the galaxy that I hadn't noticed what was happening elsewhere. The surface in front of me swept down, underneath the bottom half of the galaxy. Above us, the surface continued above the galaxy; a mirror image of the surface below, encasing the whole structure. All around the giant room at the same level at which we stood were other openings from the exhibition areas like the one we had come through.

Coming out of the openings and scattered over the entire floor and ceiling, The First stood still or floated across the vast expanse. Sparkling and shimmering in their individually crafted suits, they were their own galaxy of bright colours surrounding the brilliance of the galaxy of stars.

It was hard to tell because of the distance, but there must have been millions of The First, listening to the sounds from other worlds. What I had taken to be strange objects moving around in the galaxy close to us were actually more of The First, flying through the stars.

Why are they doing that? I asked Uncle Digit.

Inside the galaxy you can enlarge whatever you're looking at; you can watch worlds being born and stars die, and you can fly around planets or even walk across the rings of Saturn.

Gosh, can we do that?

We have to find our own sun first, Uncle Digit explained.

But you've already done this, haven't you? You know where it is?

Yes, I do.

How did you find it?

See if you can find it. Look at all of this; the billions of stars, the enormity of space. Then think about home.

I did what Uncle Digit said and thought about home in among the countless stars. I let myself drift up, Uncle Digit following close by, and together we swam through the constellations until I stopped by the light of one Sun Heart.

There you are, Uncle Digit remarked. *The Sun Heart has brought you home.*

But it's just a light. Where is the Earth and the other planets?

It's all here, but there's only room to show the larger bodies like stars and gas clouds. You just have to dig a little to find everything else.

Dig? Can I do this?

You probably could, but we have to do more than that to see your grandfather's memories. Up to now, you have been controlling everything and I've just been following.

Really?

Yes, really. Apart from the few things I showed you, you brought us here all by yourself. It's quite something, I can tell you. But I will need to take us from here if we are to go further.

I tried not to sound disappointed. *Okay.*

Remember, you will be seeing the world through your grandfather's eyes and feel things that he felt. I will control as much of it as I can, but it will feel very strange. Let me know if you're uncomfortable with anything you're experiencing.

All right.

Okay then, here we go.

The stars moved further apart as Uncle Digit expanded the area of the galaxy we were in and we flew through the solar system. We walked along the rings of Saturn and skated across the red sands of Mars before we stopped and I found myself looking down on the Earth; a blue and green ball covered in swirls of clouds standing out against the blackness.

Image after image flooded my vision as Uncle Digit began searching his father's memories. I saw the countryside, cities and roads. I saw parts of my own town with the streets full of people going about their tasks. Everything looked different, though, as if I were watching an old film. I saw ships and aeroplanes from World War Two. I saw sailors running around or below decks, eating and laughing. At one point there were flames and the screams of men.

Are you all right, Finn?

Yes, I replied.

Nearly there.

Then we were back in my own town again. I recognised my house, but it wasn't the same. The curtains were thick and dark, the door was a different colour with peeling paint and there were no flowers in the front garden.

Then the images stopped flashing past and I found myself standing in a pub.

Part 4: Alfred
Chapter 19
The Captain and the Whiskey Glass

I was standing.

I was standing up on two legs.

I could feel all the way down to my toes. I could feel the weight of my body being supported by my legs.

It was as if I was actually there. I sensed all the sights, sounds and smells around me. I felt the rough wooden surface of the bar beneath my hands. I was anxious and fiddled nervously with the wedding band on my left hand, then did the same with the signet ring on my right. I realised that I felt like this a lot of the time.

Part of me was trying to get used to these sensations, but I remembered that it was normal and that I had walked here by myself from work on the way home. It was something I did most days, even though being here seemed to make me tense.

A pint of beer was placed in front of me and I looked at the barman and smiled my thanks.

The beer smelt sour and unpleasant, but I took a sip. It tasted dark and bitter, but I enjoyed it and I felt myself relax.

I looked around the room at the other men drinking. I knew most of them and gave a small nod to one or two as they met my gaze.

On one table, two men I didn't recognise were having what looked like a heated discussion.

A small man with his back to me was talking to a larger man siting opposite him. The larger man had a full beard and moustache and a woollen cap on his head. His eyes were narrowed as he listened to the smaller man; it was clear he didn't like what was being said to him. When he replied, his voice was loud and strident. I could hear the anger, even though they weren't speaking in English.

The small man said something that made the larger man glare back and hold onto the table, as if to stop himself from leaping up and striking the other man. The small man finished his drink and put the empty glass back down on the table. There was a pause during which neither man spoke, then the larger man seemed to relax and raised himself up from the seat. He looked as though he was going to offer the smaller man his hand but he stopped and put both hands on the table, looking down on the other man.

The small man stood up as well and they stared at each other until Alfred wondered if they were going to start a fight. Then the small man abruptly turned round and left the pub. The large man remained standing to watch the other go. He sensed Alfred looking at him and glared back for a few seconds before sinking back into his seat, staring down at the drink between his hands.

"Buy you a pint, Alfred?" said a man who had come up to

the bar.

"No, thanks, Ben, just got one," I said, turning to speak to him. "Can I get you one?"

"You're all right, Alfred, thanks," said Ben. "Me and the crew are just on the way out."

"You be gone long?"

"Just a week or two," Ben said. "Got to take some crockery to Egypt."

We both gave a little laugh.

"Well, you be careful out there, I said.

"Thanks. The boys want to ... you know... before they go out ..." He trailed off awkwardly.

"That's fine, Ben."

Ben turned to a table of four men and nodded. The men got up and came towards them. I held out my hand, saying the name of each man as I shook their hand. "Abel. Michael. Sean. David. See you return safe now, boys." The five men walked past me towards the door, each one laying a hand on my shoulder as they went.

This time it was my turn to feel that I was being watched. I looked round to see the large man staring at me with interest.

I turned back to face the row of bottles behind the bar and continued drinking slowly. I was just finishing my beer when the large man came up to the bar next to me and put his glass on the counter.

"Whiskey, please." The voice was rough and deep with

hints of Scandinavia. The man paid for his drink and then turned sideways to face me, leaning against the counter with one arm. I tensed slightly, knowing what was coming next.

"You're Alfred Starling, aren't you?" said the man. I looked round at the sea-worn face, carved by the sun and storms. The small green eyes looked at me with curiosity, but held none of the anger that had been present a few minutes earlier.

"What of it?" I asked.

"I've heard of you," the man said simply. "What's the story? You were shipwrecked twice in the war. The last time you were one of only five survivors of the *HMS Stanford*; a cruiser with a crew of over seven hundred men. You were a radio operator in the middle of the ship, yet somehow you managed to escape."

I searched for any sign that I was being mocked, but the man's face was open and honest and seemed merely inquisitive.

The man took off his woollen cap, revealing a mass of tight curls, and extended his hand. "Nils Morgensen, captain of *The Daedalus*."

I took the hand that he offered me. "The Daedalus? I've not come across her. Where are you headed?"

"The Arctic."

"The Arctic? What on earth for?"

"It is a joint Danish and British scientific venture to measure the movements of glaciers and take ice samples."

The slightly clipped and straightforward manner in which the captain spoke gave his sentences a mundane feel, as if he were describing going to a grocer to buy some vegetables.

"It sounds like a long trip."

"This is just a preliminary expedition for three months."

"What do you hope to achieve by doing this?" I asked.

"I don't know. I'm not a scientist. I just know the sea and the ice."

I said nothing further, waiting to hear what else the captain might say.

"You're still looking at me suspiciously," continued the captain. "I didn't want to talk to you about your experience."

"No?" I said.

"Those of us who survived; we have all seen and done things that will never leave us. If we want to talk about them, we talk. If we don't, we don't."

I nodded and relaxed. "So, what do you want?"

The captain paused. "We are a superstitious lot, don't you think?" he continued.

"We?"

"Sailors."

"I'm not a sailor; I work in insurance."

"But you know the sea. You were a sailor. You're famous here as a sailor and this is where you choose to come. You could go to any pub in town, but you come here."

"That may be so, but I am no longer a sailor."

"Yes. I heard that you vowed never to set foot on a ship again."

"That is correct."

"They also say that no crew who has shaken your hand has been lost. And you; you survived where no one would have dreamt it was possible. Do these things not make you superstitious?"

"No, they just make me grateful. And no crew has been lost here in the five years since the war ended, whether they have shaken my hand or not."

"But yet, you still let them shake your hand."

I stared back at my empty glass.

"Maybe you need them as much as they need you?" the captain said.

I turned back sharply to look at the captain. "Maybe. But if I can help make their lives on the water even the slightest bit easier; make them forget the risks and the horrors that the sea can bring, then I feel that I'm doing something for them."

"That you're repaying your debt?" The captain's voice was gentle, but I felt uncomfortable being questioned like this.

"Something like that," I growled back.

"Does it help?" asked the captain.

I searched the captain's face again. What did this man want? Why was he asking such questions of someone he'd only just met?

I looked away and remained silent. I had been expecting

the captain to go, but he remained where he was, letting the silence hang, and I didn't want to be the one to leave.

"I want you to join my crew and come with us," the captain said eventually.

I laughed. "You want me to come with you?"

"Yes."

"Why would I do that?"

"Do you believe in fate, Mr. Starling?" he asked.

"Fate? No, not fate. I believe in luck."

"Well, here I am. I've just lost my radio operator and first mate and I find myself standing next to a radio operator who also happens to be Alfred Starling. I know you have the experience to be a first mate. This seems like too much of a coincidence to me."

"Or maybe that's all it is: a lucky coincidence."

"Yes, maybe that's all it is. Maybe I want to believe it is intended in some way because I need you. But maybe you need this as much as you need to feel you're helping these sailors here."

"I need it? I need to leave my family and come with you?"

"Yes," the captain stated.

I wanted him to leave now and was about to ask him to do so when he spoke again.

"You have a dark soul, Alfred Starling," he said.

"A dark soul," I repeated, weighing the words carefully, trying to fathom their meaning. "What makes you say that?"

178

"I've seen it before; in the eyes of men who can't forget; in the weight of the memories that smother them, suffocating them and stopping them from living."

Again, I wondered what gave this man the right to talk to me in this way.

"You think you know how I feel about everything that has happened to me? You think you know what it means to lose all your friends? And do you think that forgetting is something that just happens? That the memories will simply slip away over time and leave me in peace?"

"No, I don't think that. I know that the memories never leave you."

"Really? And what are your memories?"

"I fought in the Danish resistance. I did things I find hard to justify now. I lost friends and family. Everyone did. I was lucky, like you; I escaped and came here. I don't forget either."

"But you don't have a 'dark soul'?" I said dryly.

"The man that just left me, Henning. We have known each other since we were children. We fought together in the resistance. We survived and escaped together. We have saved each other's lives more times than you can imagine. We have clung onto each other when the nightmares became too much. We stopped each other from falling too far into a place from which we knew we would not return. Yet now we argue like a married couple and let each other down. We do that because we have healed the wounds of everything that we did and that

179

happened to us and we accept the scars that remain. We have moved on."

I didn't say anything and the captain continued.

"But you are torn. You won't return to the sea, yet you haunt this pub like a ghost. A pub full of seamen. Men who come and go with stories of the sea that you listen to in the half-light of another world."

"Enough!" I said loudly.

Voices stopped and heads turned to see what was happening, but my eyes remained on the captain and the heads turned back to resume their conversations.

"You have made your point," I said sternly. I took a few breaths to calm myself. "Perhaps there's something in what you have said, but you will still have to find another first mate."

I wanted to walk away, but I found myself unable to move, transfixed, waiting to hear what else this strange man might say.

The captain finished his whiskey and nodded to the barman for another. He paid for the drink and picked up the glass, moving the contents slowly round, watching as the amber liquid formed a small whirlpool. Without taking his eyes from the movement in the glass, he carried on speaking.

"When you're out at sea in a storm, you know you have no power over the weather. You just do everything that you can to get through. Imagine that you were inside this glass being washed around by the movement. You might think that the same thing was happening and respond in the same way, as if you had no control. But really, it is just my hand moving the glass."

"If I was in that glass I would have no control over your hand."

"That is true, but when you have a storm going on inside you, it is no different. You feel that you're powerless against the forces trying to drag you down. It is easy to think that the storm is everything; that it is beyond your control. But you just need to find the hand that is moving the glass."

"And you think you know what is causing my storm; my dark soul?"

The captain turned to face me. "Only you know that. All I've found is that to overcome it, you have to face what you fear."

"And I do that by coming with you on your expedition?"

"Yes."

I shook my head and gave a small laugh. "You have a strange way of trying to recruit people, Captain."

"Possibly. But something tells me that we need each other for this. I will be here for the next two nights, then I must leave."

I stood away from the bar and turned to go.

"Please don't wait for me," I said as I left.

Chapter 20

Lily

It was still light as I walked home, my thoughts swirling like the whiskey in the captain's glass.

When I got home I spoke to Lily, telling her everything that had happened to me in the pub and my strange meeting with the captain. Lily listened carefully, gently rubbing her slightly swollen tummy.

She didn't say anything as I recounted my story. When I had finished she remained silent, stroking her belly while I stood waiting for her to say something.

"So, do you want to go with him?" Lily said after a minute's thought.

"No, Lily. I told him that I wouldn't."

"Do you think there is anything in what he said?"

"Even if there was, I wouldn't leave you and Henry. Not now; not when we're going to have another baby."

Lily nodded. "What if you needed to go away, though?" she asked. "What if you needed to go back to the sea, to be able to free yourself?"

"Free myself?" There was irritation in my voice.

"Yes."

"You're beginning to sound like the captain," I said bitterly.

"What if he's right?" Lily's voice sounded urgent and

strained. "Alfred, it's been six years since you got back from the war and you still can't sleep through the night. You still cry and shout when you dream and you still have fits of anger that terrify me and Henry."

I moved forward and gently held onto Lily, my brow furrowed in concern.

"You're frightened of me?"

"Yes, I am. Sometimes I am."

"But why didn't you say something?"

"I couldn't, Alfred. Each time I tell myself that it's the last time, that you're getting better and putting everything behind you. I've tried to understand what it's like for you, but I can't; you don't talk to me about it. And what about Henry? He only knows you as you are now. I want your children to know the man I married."

"So do I, Lily. I don't know what to do, but I'm not sure that leaving you to go on this expedition is the answer."

"If there's any chance that going on this expedition will bring you back, then I would rather take the chance now, because in five months' time you won't be able to."

"But Lily, I don't know if I can. I don't know if I can get on a ship again."

"I think that's what the captain meant. You have to make yourself do this."

"And what if something happens? What if I don't come back? What will you do?"

There were tears in Lily's eyes as she smiled up at me. "But you're Alfred Starling. You always come back."

I struggled with my decision over the next day. I went to work and spoke to the owners of the company to see if they would give me the time off, which they would if I thought that it would help me. I checked that my life insurance was valid for such a trip. I looked up details about the ship, the captain and the expedition. I pored over maps and charts to calculate the distances, times, weather patterns and forecasts. As I did all this, I felt a little life re-enter me; a nervous anticipation and an excitement that I hadn't experienced for many years. I realised that my mind was made up and that I had come to terms with what this meant.

On the way home I went to the pub and spoke to the captain, accepting his offer. The captain gave a wry smile and shook my hand, then I went straight home.

I packed that evening and the next day spent a good deal of time with Henry, playing with him and reading to him. When I put him to bed I told him that I would be going away on an adventure and that he must look after his mother while I was away.

The next morning I said goodbye to Lily and headed off to the ship with my kit bag.

Chapter 21

Storm

The Daedalus was a small military supply vessel that had been altered with a toughened bow and an ice-breaker. A large cabin had also been constructed in front of the bridge for the scientists.

My mood dropped the instant I boarded the ship.

A tall, thin lad took my kit bag from me and I immediately lost myself in my duties getting the ship underway. As I moved about the vessel, I introduced myself to the crew, although I was nervous and apprehensive and found it hard to say more than a gruff 'hello'.

There were eleven of us, including myself. In the bridge with the captain was the second mate Jacob McCallan, a small, stout Scot with a large ginger beard and an easy smile who shook my hand warmly as I introduced myself. I climbed down the steps from the bridge into the large cabin where the four scientists were stowing and securing their equipment and documentation. There were two Englishmen, Harold Bennet and Malcolm Tailor, and two Danes, Bjarne Olap and Eric Madsen. I was grateful that they were too busy to do more than give me their names in reply to my greeting and I climbed down the steps to the sleeping cabins that had been built into the storage section below decks. It was here, inside the belly of the ship, with no view of the outside world that I had to catch myself from falling. There were more steps leading down to the engine room, but I had little appetite for descending any further at the moment. I held onto the walls and doors along the passage and walked unsteadily to the stores and galley at the far end.

I heard the galley crew before I saw them: a broad Yorkshire accent loudly giving someone advice. "Thas ganna regret stowin' that thee-er lad. F'st big wave, sum'un'll get a reet sore 'ed, an' I dunt wan' it ta be me!"

I looked round the right-hand door into the galley. A large, middle-aged man with ruddy features was helping the young man who had taken my kit bag to pack some cooking equipment safely in a high locker.

The large man turned when he saw me and walked forwards, holding out a plump hand for me to shake.

"Tha must be Alfred Starlin', our new f'st mate," he said, pleasantly. I nodded, shaking his hand. "A've 'eard o' thee," he continued, still shaking my hand. "Am Dan Sykes. Pleasure to have thee on board."

"Thank you," I muttered, disengaging my hand. I looked in the direction of the young man.

"'E's Ralph Ferguson," Sykes said. "He dunt talk much, but 'e's a good lad. Smashin' fiddle player."

"Can I see the stores?" I asked him, feeling the need to get back on deck as quickly as possible.

"Aye," he replied, moving past me and opening the door opposite.

Whoever was paying for the trip wasn't stinting on the food. There were cans to last a few months, bags of rice and flour as well as a stack of fresh vegetables. I could see crates of oranges and apples and what looked like dried meats carefully wrapped in cloth. Sykes was looking at me expectantly.

"I'm impressed," I said, truthfully.

"Aye. Ye can look t'ave some good grub," he said, smiling.

"These are the forward stores?" I asked, pointing at a door between the galley and the food store that led into the bows of the ship.

"Aye," he replied, "An' there's t'other store in t'aft, under the captain's cabin."

I opened the door.

"I'll let thee check 'em out tha self, sir," he said, moving back into the galley.

"Thanks," I said, looking inside and starting to count the life-jackets, lamps and other equipment there. Once I had finished, I walked back along the passage to the steps and peered down into the murky twilight of the engine room. The gentle thrum of the idling engine was strangely comforting and allowed me to steady myself before I climbed down.

Two men with oil-smeared faces and clothes stopped what they were doing and looked to see who had joined them. They didn't say anything. The one I took to be the engineer tilted his head slightly in a questioning manner. The one I took to be the stoker was chewing on a piece of wood, the end of which protruded from his mouth like a cigarette. One of his hands was on a valve near to the boiler and he had small, sharp eyes that stared at me as though I were no more than an interesting distraction from his duties.

"I'm Alfred Starling," I said.

Neither man made a move.

"Per Anders," the engineer said at length, in a thick Danish accent. "That's Jens Pedersen," he added, indicating the stoker. "His English is not good."

"Pleased to meet you," I responded.

"You must be Henning's replacement," Anders stated.

"Yes, I…" my words were drowned out by a sudden blast of steam as Pedersen turned the level he was holding to release the pressure in the boiler.

It was clear I wasn't entirely welcome in their world, so I nodded to both men briefly and made my way thankfully back up the steps until I was out in the air once more.

I kept myself busy until the ship got underway and took the first night watch to tire myself as much as possible before staggering off to bed in the early hours of the morning, falling asleep almost immediately.

I woke up shortly afterwards with a sharp cry, covered in sweat.

The Danish scientist in the cabin next to me, Bjarne Olap, stuck his head round my door.

"Are you okay?" he asked, concerned.

"Yes," I said. "Thank you."

I was embarrassed that I had woken everyone, and I took my bedding and went up to sleep among the tables and cabinets in the large cabin.

Being at sea began to relax me though and after a few days the crew were amused when I announced, rather grumpily, that it was too cold in the research cabin and I was going to move back into my own cabin below.

I started chatting more easily, making the crew laugh and raising their spirits. We talked about our experiences and, although it was hard, I was able to tell the crew what had happened at sea and how it had affected me. They shared their own stories and I found comfort in the telling and sharing of experiences.

Two weeks into the journey, I was leaning on the ship's rail looking out to sea. The captain came and stood next to me and we watched the ship moving through the water.

"You see that we are getting more sea-ice now?" he said, pointing out the large lumps surrounding us.

"Yes, it's increasing quite a lot."

"We are nearly there. It will only be another day or two."

I nodded and carried on staring out.

"How are you getting on?" he asked.

189

A week ago I would have found this question intrusive, but I took it in the spirit of companionship and concern in which it was asked.

"I feel more myself. I didn't believe you, but I suppose I should thank you for asking me to join you."

"Don't thank me yet," said the captain. "This is the easy part, where you feel you have started to get your life back. There will be hard times ahead, but I think you will have more strength to deal with those now."

I stared back out to sea. There was a strong wind and a medium swell. I enjoyed the feeling of the air rushing through my hair and the long rising and falling of the boat. As we got to the top of one crest I thought I saw a dark line on the horizon and turned to the captain.

"What do you think to that, Captain?" I asked, pointing towards the line. "There was nothing in the forecast."

The captain looked where I pointed and we both watched the line between the rises of the boat. The line was getting thicker with each rise. After a few minutes we looked at each other with alarm.

The captain left to go to the bridge and I immediately went down to warn the crew and the scientists to tie everything down before joining the captain on the bridge. I radioed our position and looked at the charts to see if there was anywhere we could head to if needed.

The wind was already picking up and the storm line was

thickening. "How long do you think before it hits us, Captain?" asked McCallan, the second mate.

"Twenty minutes at most. Alfred, can you see anywhere for us?"

I pointed at the chart. "There's a bay here, but we would be heading into more ice and it would take us more than half an hour at this speed."

"That's okay," responded the captain. "She's good for at least a foot of ice, maybe more." The captain opened the speaking tube, shouted something in Danish to the engine room then turned back to me. "The engines are from a bigger boat, so I'm hoping there will be more than enough power for us. Take the heading from Alfred, Jacob."

I gave the second mate the heading and the boat turned away from the storm and started to speed up. It was now a race to see if we could get to land before the storm.

"I'm going to check with everyone again," I told the captain.

I headed down the stairs to see if the scientists were all right, then carried on down to secure all the cabins and check in on the galley and the crew members there. I moved further down into the ship to the engine room, and asked if the crew there had everything they needed. Then I made my way back up to the bridge.

It was now possible to make out a coastline of rough ragged peaks covered in snow. After a further ten minutes, the gap in the mountains to the shelter of the bay was clearly visible. The wind was sweeping in behind us, making the ship rattle and whine, as anything that protruded from the surface was struggling not to be ripped from its footing by the force of the gale. A rope that hadn't been tied down was whipped up into the air and began flailing around like a crazed snake. There were occasional bangs as pieces of sea-ice were picked up by the wind and smashed against the boat; one piece struck the bridge directly behind us. We could see that the storm was nearly on top of us and the captain again shouted something down to the engine room before moving to take the wheel from the second mate.

"Hold onto something, gentlemen!" he shouted.

Then it became impossible to hear anything but the howling of the wind. The sea washed over the bridge as we rode through the water and we caught only the occasional glimpse of the opening we were heading for as we reached the top of each mountainous wave. A chunk of ice smashed through one of the thick pieces of glass and fell onto the console to the right of the captain, breaking one of the instruments there. The rain was streaming in through the opening and the noise was all but deafening.

As we got closer to the bay, the headland slowly began to protect us. The size of the waves decreased and the boat was pushed towards the opening by the wind and the tide. The mountains on either side of the entrance rose spectacularly to great heights, like stern guardians ushering us into some forgotten realm.

Up until then, the ship had been ploughing through broken sea-ice, but as we passed between the giant portals, the ice sheet was intact and the bow cut through it with a sound like rifles being fired. The captain guided the ship further in, to a place completely sheltered from the storm, and called a full stop.

"We will rest up here for a day or two to make repairs," he announced. "Alfred, radio base and let them know where we are and what has happened."

I had been working on the radio and I turned to the captain. "It must have been damaged in the storm. I'll see what I can do."

The captain and second mate left the bridge to check on the ship and the crew. After half an hour, I still hadn't got the radio working and threw the spanner I was holding away from me in frustration. I suddenly felt very isolated and decided to go out on deck to join the men who were leaning against the gunwales, looking out into the bay. We were silent for a while, gazing at the great sweep of mountains that surrounded the expanse of snow-covered ice through which we had travelled. Although the rain had stopped, there was still a strong wind blowing over the peaks and we could see great puffs of snow being whipped off the sides and the tops of the mountains.

"Pretty inhospitable place," observed the scientist,

Malcolm Tailor.

I looked at him with surprise. "I think it's beautiful. Anyway, I thought you would be used to this," I said.

Bjarne Olap, laughed. "He's just a lab boy. He's never been on a field trip before, but he'll get used to it. It's going to be far colder where we're headed."

"The snow looks really flat," I commented to Olap. "Is that normal? It seems so perfectly smooth it looks almost unreal."

"It does, doesn't it," Olap replied. "Maybe there's very little or no wind down here. It seems unnaturally quiet."

I leaned over the gunwale to look at the surface next to the boat. "It goes right up to the boat," I said. "Look. It's like we've just been put here. You can't even see where the ice has broken."

Olap leaned over and looked as well. He grunted and was about to comment on it when there was a shout from further down the gunwale that made both of us turn round to see what was happening. The two Danes from the engine room were having a discussion. Pedersen, the stoker, was clearly excited about something; he was pointing out into the snow and shouting to Anders. Then Pedersen rushed back into the main cabin and down the stairs to below decks.

"What's got into Pedersen?" I asked Olap.

"He says he saw some polar bears out there."

"Polar bears?" I said in surprise. "I've never seen polar

bears before." I looked out to where Pedersen had been pointing. "He must have very good eyes – I can't see anything."

"He has," replied Olap. "He's a hunter."

After a few minutes, Pedersen came running back up with a rifle in his hands and returned to his position next to his engine room companion.

"What's he going to do?" I asked. "Surely he's not going to shoot them?"

"He is a hunter," said Olap with an amused expression. "That's what they do."

"I don't think shooting a creature from the side of a ship can be classed as hunting."

"Maybe not to you, but Pedersen has different ideas about that sort of thing."

I turned away. "I've got a radio to fix," I said and headed back up to the bridge, my mood slightly spoiled.

Chapter 22
The Light where Memories End

I left the door open and my spirits improved as I listened to the crew talking and laughing while I worked on the radio. I found the sounds on-board ship were once again providing the comfort and the sense of kinship that I valued and that formed the reassuring bond between myself and life at sea. There were still resonances of other, more disturbing sounds, but these were more distant and indistinct. I could get close to them if I chose, but they were no longer the constant, unbidden first thoughts of my mind.

I had been working for quarter of an hour when the sounds outside took on a different tone. I could hear voices raised in both English and Danish and then the captain's strident voice rising above them. There was a sharp cry followed by a short silence before everyone started talking at the same time.

I ran out and down the stairs. Pedersen was sitting on the deck, wiping a bloodied nose with his sleeve while the captain stood over him holding the rifle.

"Is everything all right, Captain?" I asked with concern.

"It's all right, Alfred. I was just explaining to Pedersen that I didn't want the first act of the crew of this ship to be one of butchery."

The captain gave the rifle to McCallan. "See that this is

locked away until it is actually needed."

McCallan nodded to the captain and went inside. The captain helped Pedersen up and spoke to him in English. "All right, then. Let's see how strange these bears of yours are, shall we?"

I moved next to Olap again. "What does he mean 'strange'?"

"Pedersen was saying that he'd never seen a male polar bear walking with his cubs and their mother before. He says it's really unusual and that they would all make a fine trophy."

I could see the group of bears clearly now. They were strolling towards us in a leisurely manner with the cubs stopping to play and fight for a short time before running to catch up with their mother. "My God, he was going to shoot the cubs and the mother as well?" I said to Olap.

"We were all trying to persuade him otherwise, but like I said, he sees things differently and he was determined. The captain eventually asked him to hand over the rifle, but he was getting worked up, saying that this was once in a lifetime, and… well, you saw the result."

I looked back at the bears. "They look like they're headed for us. Is that usual?"

Olap thought for a few moments before answering. "Polar bears are often very curious and will want to investigate. In my experience, though, this would not be true of a group that included cubs."

"So, you agree with Pedersen that something is odd?"

"Yes, I do."

Everyone was now watching the group of bears as they walked closer. They got to about fifty yards of the boat and then stopped. The two adult bears started swaying their heads around and then lifted themselves on to their back legs.

"It looks like they are trying to smell us," said Pedersen.

But they weren't sniffing. They opened their mouths and produced sounds that filled the air with a wailing and unearthly melody.

I looked round at Pedersen. "What are they doing?"

"Are they singing?" asked Olap.

"I've not heard anything like it before," replied Pedersen.

And then everyone cried out. I covered my ears and groaned. Something was inside my head. A storm was blowing through my mind, picking up images from my past and bowling them along like leaves stripped from an autumn tree.

I looked around at the others to see if they felt the same. Everyone else was staring from person to person with surprise and amazement on their faces, but with no sign of alarm or concern.

The constant flow of memories was making me feel dizzy and I wanted them to stop.

I groaned again more intensely and dropped to my hands and knees, squeezing my eyes shut and clenching and unclenching my fingers.

My mind was full of images from the war, from my ship; memories that I had learnt to push away; memories that took me into darkness.

The outside world on board *The Daedalus* became more distant as the chaos of memories roaring through me began to converge, and the sights, sounds and smells of a naval engagement became starkly clear. I saw myself in the radio control room of *HMS Stanford*. I could feel the shake of the ship as the guns pounded and could hear the fierce shriek and burst of the shells. I was trying to relay to the captain the latest order that had come through from the fleet commander, but the internal communications were down and I rushed from the room with the orders in my hand.

I was climbing the stairs to the next deck and was halfway up when the explosion happened. I knew instantly that a shell or torpedo had penetrated through the hull and detonated one of the magazines. The blast threw me back down the stairs, and I landed on a sailor who had been following me. I quickly got to my feet and leant down to help the other man. A second explosion ripped through the ship. The sailor was hurled away from me and I fell down a now sloping corridor and came to rest heavily against the door at the end. Fire penetrated through the gloom and the screaming of tortured metal filled my ears as the ship tore itself apart.

Then I saw something I didn't recognise.

I always remembered the flashes and the noise, the terror

I felt as I watched the water appearing suddenly from everywhere, but I had never remembered what had happened after that and could never tell people how I had escaped from where I had been in the ship.

But here was that moment; the moment where the memories ended.

Through the rushing water and the semi-darkness I could see a light coming towards me. The panic I had been feeling subsided, even as the water closed in over my head. I watched as the light came up to my face and stopped for a few moments before moving away from me again. I knew that the ship was sinking, but there was no increase in pressure and I had no desire to breathe. I could feel myself being pulled forwards, floating through corridors, passed ruptured walls and out into the sea, leaving the broken vessel to fall to the depths as I rose up to the surface.

As I watched myself following the light to the safety of the air above the sea, I could feel all the other forces that were in my mind moving away and out of my head until I found I could open my eyes again and look at my hands on the deck in front of me. I gasped like a man who had been struggling for breath. What did all this mean? Why was I remembering everything now? Was it real, or was I just filling in the gaps in my memory with something fanciful?

Chapter 23
Leaving The Ship

Around me I could hear the others talking.

I heard Tailor saying, "I can't hear the singing anymore," and someone else replying, "No, neither can I. I can see... I can hear... words. But, that's impossible."

I heard the captain say, "Are they talking to us? How is this happening?"

There was a lot of talking, then Tailor said loudly, "Listen. They're saying hello. I heard the word 'Greetings'."

"Yes," I heard Bennet, the other English scientist, agree.

"I heard the Danish word for 'hello'," said Olap. "How can we hear the same thing in English and Danish?"

Ferguson, the galley hand, suddenly shouted out excitedly, "They're telling us their names, I think! Yes, listen. Wind Over Mountain. One of them is called Wind Over Mountain."

Everyone was saying, "Yes, Wind Over Mountain and Wind Over Sea," and telling each other the names. Someone said, "Jens, you were going to shoot a bear with a name," and everyone laughed.

I shook my head and got to my feet unsteadily. Everyone was grouped together, looks of amazement on their faces, each one asking another if they were all hearing the same things.

No one looked at me or showed any interest in what had happened to me.

Then the captain held his hand up and asked for quiet. "They are saying something else." Everyone stopped speaking and listened to the singing.

"They want us to come with them," said the captain.

"Yes, to show us something," said Pedersen.

"Or take us to someone," someone else volunteered.

The talking started up again and the captain raised his voice to be heard above everyone. "Quiet." He waited for everyone to stop talking. "So, what do you think we should do? Do you think we should go with them?"

I watched in disbelief as everyone nodded vigorously and talked excitedly about where they might be going.

I went up to speak to Olap, but he brushed past me saying that he had to get ready to leave. Everyone else rushed around as well, and then there was just myself and the captain left on the deck. The captain was standing by the gunwale, staring out at the polar bears. As I moved towards him the captain turned to me with a slightly confused look on his face.

"Alfred?"

"Yes, Captain."

"Why are you still here? Why aren't you getting ready?"

"Surely you're not going to go down there, Captain, and walk off into god knows where with a couple of polar bears?"

"But they're talking to us, Alfred. They want to take us to

see someone."

"Captain. There are no words. There are just strange noises. It must be a trick or some kind of illusion."

"A trick?" the captain asked hesitantly.

"Yes. You can't seriously believe that bears can talk."

The captain didn't say anything. He was still looking at me as if he wasn't sure why I was there. I softened my voice. "Just stay on the boat, please, Captain. You have to stay on the boat. Wait for a while and see what happens."

"But why, Alfred? Why is it only you that can't hear anything?"

"I don't know. I thought I could to start with. It felt like something was trying to get inside my head, but it's gone now."

"You felt something trying to get inside your head?"

"Yes, I think so."

"Now you're sounding fanciful, Alfred."

"But there's something wrong here, Captain. It can't be real."

"Who knows what is real, Alfred? You may stay on the boat if you wish, but I'm going with my crew."

By now, the rest of the crew were running back up on deck with additional clothing for the snow. They headed for the stern of the boat and started to make their way down the ladder. McCallan gave the captain a large overcoat, which he put on. Then the captain followed everyone off the boat without another word while I, pacing back and forth in indecision, watched them go.

The bears were already walking slowly away and didn't seem very interested in the line of men who were following them. I watched them for a minute, then went back up to the bridge to grab my coat before dashing to the back of boat and down the ladder. Then I ran through the snow until I caught up with the captain.

The captain looked round at me, panting to get my breath back. "So, you decided to come, Alfred?"

"Yes," I said, breathing heavily. "I didn't think I should miss this, really."

"I'm glad you changed your mind."

I stared back at the deserted ship. "I presume the ship's pretty safe where it is. It seems wrong leaving her all alone."

"She'll be all right," said the captain without looking back.

Then I noticed something.

"Captain. Look, there are no tracks."

"No tracks, Alfred? Where?"

"We're not leaving any tracks. The snow looks untouched. Take a look."

The captain turned to look back the way they had come. "I'm sure there's an explanation."

"But Captain, it can't be normal. Can't you see how the snow forms back up after we have walked across it?"

The captain looked round at him with an uncharacteristic smile on his face.

"No, not really."

"Look at young Ferguson ahead of us there," I said, pointing at the man directly in front of us. "His footprints disappear as he moves forward."

The captain looked at the rising and falling of the feet in front of him. He seemed to get lost somewhere in the movement, his eyes fixed on the feet as they moved, but without being really focused on them.

"What do you think, Captain?" I asked after a minute.

The captain stirred. "Yes. It's rather unusual, isn't it?"

"Unusual?"

The captain had stopped staring at the feet in front of him now and was gazing about as before.

"Yes. Well, snow doesn't normally do that, does it?" he said in an off-hand way. "Maybe it's a new kind of snow."

It was as though he was in a dream and just accepting everything that happened as real rather than trying to make sense of what he was experiencing.

"And you still don't think it odd that we are following a couple of polar bears?"

"They seem to want us to go with them. I don't think they mean us any harm. They told us that they don't want to eat us."

I gave a small chuckle. "They told you that, did they?"

"Yes, they did."

"And that's okay with you? A polar bear tells you it doesn't want to eat you and you believe it?"

The captain seemed unaffected by my sarcasm. "They said that they want us to meet someone. Something to do with the sun, I think."

"And in your experience, how common is it to have a conversation with a polar bear?"

The captain paused and seemed to consider this. "It's not something that I've come across before," he said.

I was finding it hard to know what to say. "Not come across before? Captain, this isn't an interesting new orchid you happen to have discovered. This is something that is clearly impossible."

"But how can it be impossible, Alfred? Everyone heard them say the same things. You're the only one who didn't hear them."

"That's right, I didn't. But can't you hear yourself, Captain? You don't sound like yourself."

The captain stopped and turned, looking at me intently for the first time. "You're right, Alfred. I don't sound like myself."

I sighed, relieved that I had finally managed to get through to him.

"Well, do you think there's something else going on here?" I said.

"I don't really know," the captain replied. Then he breathed in deeply and smiled. "I feel different as well. Actually, I feel better than I've felt for a long time. I feel so good I want to sing." He laughed a deep rolling laugh that I hadn't heard before and gave me a slap on the back that nearly took me off my feet.

"You want to sing?" I asked hopelessly.

"Yes."

There didn't seem to be anything else to add, so I remained silent and walked along beside the captain, watching carefully for anything to indicate what was going to happen next. Ferguson was holding something under his arm that I hadn't spotted before. I turned to the captain.

"Has Ferguson brought his violin with him?" I asked in a slightly resigned voice.

"Yes, I think he has," the captain replied, as if it were the most natural thing in the world.

"Why would he do that?"

"You've heard him play, haven't you? He's very good."

"Well, that's obviously a good enough reason to bring a violin into a frozen wilderness."

"And I believe that Bjarne has brought his ukulele and Jens his accordion."

I looked at Olap and Pedersen walking further ahead; they too were carrying their instruments.

"Do you know when they're going to get a chance to play them?" I asked with genuine interest.

"No, but I'm sure an opportunity will arise at some point."

I stopped asking questions. There seemed little point in trying to find a rational explanation for anything. I could hear the other crew members chatting and laughing easily among themselves, as if they were having a relaxing walk in the countryside. I wondered if it might start to seem natural to me as well. That I would fall into the easy acceptance of things that were accepted as real by others; that the feeling of unreality would slowly dissolve into a state of normality, where being taken by bears to visit some unknown being was just a part of life.

I concentrated on where they were going. I could see the shoreline encircling the bay and had assumed that we were heading to some part of that and then on somewhere beyond, but instead we had turned and were headed for the part of the mountains now closest to us. Here, there was no shoreline and huge slabs of grey rock fell steeply into the frozen sea.

There didn't seem to be any obvious destination in sight. Our way continued straight on to the bottom of a very large deposit of snow that must have detached itself from the mountain above some time ago. Over the months or years it had eroded into giant columns of different lengths stretching for hundreds of yards, resembling the pipes of some enormous cathedral organ.

We walked for another ten minutes, after which we could see an opening leading into the mass of snow.

Chapter 24
Dinner and Dance

The bears stopped to one side of the opening and sat down. The larger, male bear sang and everyone said something along the lines of "Yes, we will follow the path."

I spoke to the captain, although I had little hope of a reasonable response.

"Captain. Are you happy going in there? It can't be all that safe, can it?"

The captain spoke gently. "Well, Alfred. I can't see them bringing us all this way to bury us under a mountain of snow."

I had to agree that that was one of the least likely outcomes. I sighed and carried on, but as I walked past the bears I stopped and looked at the larger male. I would probably never get the chance again, and I was fascinated to be able to see one of these majestic animals at such close quarters. I wanted to reach out and touch it, but the bear stared at me in a way left left no doubt it would not end well if I tried.

"Alfred! We're waiting for you," the captain called.

I turned away from the bear and headed into the passage with the others. The crew had stopped chatting now and were silent as they moved forward.

The walls were gently curved to form a rounded ceiling and there was light coming from somewhere – whether from the passageway itself or from some other source, I couldn't tell. It was much warmer than I would have expected from being inside a mound of snow, and as I walked along I took one of my gloves off and ran my fingers along the wall. The surface was cool to the touch and perfectly smooth, like polished metal. It was definitely not made of snow.

We had not travelled very far when the passageway turned and opened up into a large circular chamber filled with the same soft light as the passage. Filling the room like the light, and also with no discernible source, was a high-pitched wavering sound, like someone trying and failing to find the right radio frequency.

Protruding at regular intervals along the curve of the wall to my right were eleven small empty platforms the size and height of a chair seat, smooth and white like the walls, with no indication of how they were supported. To the right of each platform and slightly above were eleven further platforms about the same size, all but one of which held a variety of food and drink.

As there were eleven of us, I presumed that there must be one chair and one food platform for each crew member and scientist. I heard the others saying things like, "Yes" and "Thank you" and then everyone made their way towards specific chairs, where they commented how all of their favourite foods and drinks were here for them.

I was left standing dumbfounded. The only other objects

visible in the room were a white cylinder about eight feet tall with a slightly tapered top and bottom and a small glowing ball of light that looked like it was suspended in mid-air a small way in front of the cylinder. I wondered if it was the ball that was producing the light and the sound.

I looked back at the men. The only unoccupied platform was nearest to me. I made my way slowly to it and sat down. The captain was next to me, holding a large glass of whiskey, which he drank down and placed back on the platform. The glass immediately refilled and the captain gave a hearty laugh, picked the glass back up and drank again, before putting the glass back down and watching it refill itself once more.

The others had also found out that all the drinks were automatically replenished and were laughing and joking together about it. It started to smell and sound very much like a pub.

The captain turned to me and looked at my empty platform.

"Don't you want anything to eat and drink, Alfred?"

"I'm not very hungry," I said truthfully. "Anyway, I don't see where I might get some food from even if I was hungry."

"You just have to ask for it."

"Ask? Ask who?" I said with genuine surprise.

"Our host here."

I felt a little alarmed. "Our host?"

"Over there," said the captain, pointing at the white

cylinder.

"That? That is our host?"

"Yes."

"What is it?"

"That, I don't know. It comes from a different planet."

"Sorry? A different planet?"

"Yes, that's what it told us."

"It told you?"

"Yes."

"How did it do that?"

"Can't you hear it?"

"No, I can't."

"I suppose if you can't hear the bears you won't be able to hear it either."

"And you believe it comes from a different planet?"

"Why wouldn't I?"

I stared at the cylinder. "Maybe I will ask it for something," I said, starting to get up.

The captain put a hand on my arm to stop me. "If you want something, Alfred, you just need to speak and it will appear. You can stay where you are."

I looked down and shook the captain's hand from my arm. "Let's assume that I don't want to stay where I am."

The captain said nothing further and turned his attention back to his food and drink.

I got up and started to walk across the room, unsure of

what I was going to do. As I got closer to the cylinder my footsteps started to drag. Each step became harder than the last until I struggled to make any ground over the short distance. I felt as though I was walking through fast-flowing water that was forcing me back. I looked at the cylinder and the glowing ball, just a few feet away.

Something told me that the force was coming from the ball. As I stared at it, straining to make headway towards it, I was struck by the thought of the light that had saved me from the ship. Was this the same light? Was this glowing ball the light that had pulled me up through a dying ship, past ruptured steel and drowning comrades? I tried to remember exactly what I had seen.

Then, like someone moving a chess piece across a board, I was pushed back along the floor and forced to sit down on the platform that served as my seat.

"You're back," said the captain, a smile breaking out on his broad face. "Just in time. Ferguson is about to play."

I couldn't hide my astonishment. "Didn't you see what just happened to me?"

"Yes. You went over there and now you are here again."

"That's all you saw?"

"Did I miss something?"

"Captain. Whatever's happening here, we're not in control of it. You must realise that now?"

"Even if that was the case, what do you propose we do?

If we have no control, surely we can't do anything about it."

"Wasn't it you that said you sometimes just have to find the hand that is moving the glass?"

"Yes, but that was different. Now I want to listen to Ferguson."

The captain turned back to the room and I had little to do but watch as events unfolded.

Ferguson stood up in front of everyone with his violin and started to play a lilting melody imbued with sadness. Even in my current state, I found myself affected by the music as it floated and soared, filling the chamber, weaving a sense of loss and longing into the minds of all those present.

I could see that the others were affected by it as well. When it was finished, a few of them wiped tears from their eyes as they clapped loudly.

Ferguson bowed, then started to play a livelier piece. It gradually sped up and as it got faster and faster several of the crew got up and danced, either singly or with each other. The captain stood up and began clapping and whooping.

I shouted over the noise. "Captain! I think it's making you do all this. I have no idea why, but there is no rational explanation for what's going on."

The captain didn't stop clapping. "It just wants us to sing and dance," he said. "There can't be any harm in that."

"Can't you see it's controlling you? Do you really want to be doing these things?"

"Yes, I do. I haven't danced this dance since I was a boy. It makes me feel young again." And the captain left to join the others wheeling about the floor.

The dance finished with raucous applause and everyone sat down again as someone else got ready to perform. I remained silent, watching the different crew members getting up to play or sing. As time went on I felt more and more drawn to the glowing ball, wondering what was really happening. Why was I the only one who couldn't hear the bears and the host? Why did I suddenly have a memory of how I had escaped from the ship? If this really was the light that had guided me to safety, why was it here now? Was I unaffected by it, or was I being controlled now just as much as the others?

Something was trying to get inside my head again. Not the same kaleidoscope of spinning images that I experienced the first time, but small tendrils, like smoke, softly penetrating my thoughts. I felt that I could easily push them away if I wanted to; that all I had to do was blink and they would leave my head. But I let them stay, inviting them to come in further, asking what they wanted of me.

And come in they did, like a thousand shafts of light suddenly erupting in my mind. I stood up in shock as my head filled with light and then watched with a mixture of horror and fascination as the glowing ball floated across the room and rested in the air two feet in front of me.

Chapter 25

Escape

The music stopped and I could see all the men looking around them and at each other with surprise and confusion. The cylinder moved swiftly across the floor and stopped with the glowing ball in between itself and me. Then the larger bear came running through the opening to the chamber and stood up on its hind feet close to the cylinder, towering over everybody, raising its head to sing.

Wind Over Mountain is here. The words rang clearly in my head.

The cylinder was making its high-pitched wavering noises, but now I could distinctly hear words.

You must give me the Sun Heart. It does not belong to you.

I stared at the cylinder, then up to the bear, then back to the cylinder again.

"What's happening?" I said, uncertainly. "I can understand you now."

You are connected to the Sun Heart, said the voice I now recognised as coming from the cylinder. *The Sun Heart is allowing you to understand what is being said.*

"The Sun Heart? Is that what you call the glowing ball?"

Yes.

"What is it?"

The Sun Heart is not something that you can understand. You must give it to me.

I looked at the glowing ball. "Give it to you?"

Yes. You just need to take it and give it to me.

My left arm was slightly raised up and I felt myself slowly moving it further towards the ball, reaching out to touch it, but something made me hesitate and I stopped myself.

"Can't you take it?" I said, carefully.

There was a moment's silence before the reply came. *No, I cannot take the Sun Heart.*

"Why not?"

Again, the reply didn't come immediately. *You are stopping me from coming any closer.*

"I'm stopping you?" I said with some surprise.

Yes.

"How am I doing that?"

I do not know.

I looked at the Sun Heart. Was it doing this? What was it? What kept it floating in the air like that?

I moved a few paces to the right and the Sun Heart followed me, keeping the same distance away. I moved back again and so did the Sun Heart. It was linked to me in some way.

"So, the Sun Heart is attached to me and you cannot take it," I said. "And without it you have no power to stop me from leaving."

The Sun Heart is not my only source of power. And you cannot leave, so you will eventually give it to me.

"Cannot leave?" I repeated.

I looked towards the opening and discovered that it was no longer there. I became confused and looked around me. I saw the captain and the men staring at me expectantly. The captain took a step forward. "Give it back, Alfred," he said urgently. The natural commanding tone of his voice was diminished and he sounded afraid and unsure. "I don't really understand what's been happening, but we all just want to go now."

"But Captain, we don't know what this creature will do to us if I give it back. Look what it made all of you do."

"It does not mean us any harm, Alfred. It will let us go."

"You know this? How can we trust it? This creature has been controlling all of you."

"That's not the point, Alfred," said the captain. "We don't have a choice now. You have to give it back."

"We always have a choice, Captain."

The captain started to move closer to me. "Come on, Alfred. Please don't make me take it from you." Some of the others were moving forward as well and I began to feel hemmed in.

"Get back, all of you!" I cried, holding my right hand out as if to fend them off.

The captain, crew and scientists were all suddenly lifted off their feet and swept back towards the wall of the chamber, together with what food and drink remained unfinished on their tables. I stared at the men in disbelief as they struggled to get up from where they had been thrown, disentangling themselves from each other.

I looked down at my right hand as if it didn't belong to me. Had I done this? There was something not quite normal about my hand. I could see what looked like a slight shadow; a blurring of the line between where my fingers ended and the space around them continued, as if my hand somehow extended beyond its natural limits.

As I gazed at my hand with growing alarm, something shifted inside me, like the world rushing back into focus after the haze of a light doze. My senses became overloaded with a flood of new information, as if there were lines flowing out from my hands, crossing and re-crossing as they stretched and spread out across the chamber, connecting everything they touched and connecting me to everything. I could feel the perfect texture of the wall and the ceiling of the chamber and even the slight changes in the temperature of the air surrounding me. As I looked back at the captain and the men I could sense all of the pain, anger, fear and confusion that was going on inside them.

Looking at my left hand, I became aware of the connections between myself and the bear and the cylinder and of the force being generated that was holding them back, stopping them from coming any closer. A force I must have instinctively created as soon as they had moved towards me, but that I didn't know I had created until now.

How was all this possible? I thought. I reeled back, overwhelmed.

Now you see why you must return the Sun Heart, said the voice of the cylinder. *You have no idea what you have.*

I took a deep breath to steady myself and searched for any sense of what was going on inside the cylinder. Although I could clearly feel the anger and growing frustration within the bear, the cylinder remained blank.

"I might not have any idea of what this is," I said. "But I'm also sure that I don't want you to have it."

As the captain has said, I am not sure you have a choice, the cylinder replied.

"We will just have to disagree on that for the moment," I replied.

I concentrated on the force holding the bear and the cylinder. I could feel a slight, almost magnetic, resistance between them and my hands. For the moment I was just holding on to it, keeping everything in place, but I was sure that I could control it, that I was able to move it and manipulate it.

I tried to draw more power from the Sun Heart by imagining the force between myself and the bear and the cylinder increasing; that it was becoming something strong enough to drive them back.

I felt a slight increase in the resistance and was surprised when they both moved away from me towards the wall of the chamber, the cylinder gracefully sliding along, the bear struggling and fighting against the force pushing him.

By this time, the captain and the others had got to their feet and made their way nervously to me.

I turned to them. "Are you all right, Captain?" I asked.

"Yes, I think so," said the captain, a little shaken. "It looks like no one is going to persuade you to give that back, so I hope you know what you're doing."

"I'd be lying to you, Captain, if I told you that I understand any of this, but I know I can get us out of here."

The captain looked at me and the Sun Heart floating in the air by my head, then over to the bear and the cylinder trapped against the wall. He nodded slowly and looked at the others, who all looked at each other before nodding in agreement. "All right, Alfred," he said. "Do whatever you need to."

I turned back to the wall where I knew the opening used to be. I could sense the thickness of the wall and the open space of the bay beyond. While keeping the bear and the cylinder against their part of the wall, I generated a force that punched a hole all the way through the wall to the air outside.

I motioned to the captain and the men to move to the hole that had been made, but no sooner were we running towards it than the material that had been pushed out gathered itself together and flew straight back in, filling the hole completely. We stood there, looking at a blank wall that once again had no sign of any opening.

The captain turned to me. "What now, Alfred?"

"I'll keep it open this time," I said calmly. "You will all have to follow me through," I added, signalling everyone to move behind me.

I waited for the men to position themselves and then I sprang forward trusting that the Sun Heart would move with me. I generated the hole as I ran and kept up a constant pressure as we moved, so that the material flying back in to refill the tunnel was continually being pushed out.

Soon we found ourselves out in the bay once more, pausing to catch our breath.

Chapter 26

Trapped

We were slightly further down from where we had entered the passage to the cave. The female bear and the cubs were a little way off, but when she saw us emerge, the female trotted towards us and we quickly continued running in the direction of the boat.

I had lost contact with the male bear and the cylinder, but I looked back to see the larger bear careering out of the opening I had made. I shouted at the men to keep going, then I stopped and turned to face the bears closing in on me.

I held my hand up and the bears slowed down and stopped a few feet in front of me.

"I have the Sun Heart," I said. "You serve me now."

The bear looked at the glowing ball, hovering just above and in front of my head, then looked back down at me.

Wind Over Mountain serves no man, he sang.

"That may be," I continued, a hard tone entering my voice, "but you know the power of the Sun Heart and you know what I can do with it if I choose to."

The bear swayed uneasily from side to side, then shuffled back uncomfortably.

Wind Over Mountain and Wind Over Sea will stay, the bear sang, with obvious reluctance.

I nodded and turned to join the others running for the ship, my mind full of doubt. I hadn't imagined that we would be free to leave so easily, but nothing hindered us as we jogged the half mile or so back to the ship. My unease grew with each step, though, and shortly before I got to the ship, I stopped. I looked at the Sun Heart, suspended in the air in front of me.

"Let's see what you can show me," I said to it under my breath. I extended my new senses over the whole bay, to see if there was anything happening; anything that would show that our host in the chamber hadn't given up.

I felt down, under the layer of unnatural snow on the surface, to the small layer of real snow beneath, then to the sea-ice, thick and solid. Then on through the sea, continuing down and down, deeper than I would have imagined. So deep, I could feel nothing but the darkness and the cold and an absolute stillness.

Then I touched something and stopped, my heart pounding. Surely nothing could be living that far down. But something was there; sleeping. Something so vast and ancient that it seemed to belong to another time. I wondered if it was under the control of the cylinder, but it had obviously been undisturbed for a very long time.

What if I woke it up? Would I be able to control it? Would I be able to use it to help us escape if I needed to?

My thoughts were broken by the roar of the ship's engines. Looking up, I saw that everyone was already back on board, busy getting everything ready. The captain was shouting orders and the men were calling to each other.

I started running, but stopped again almost immediately. My feet were no longer sinking into snow, but striking something hard. Alarmed, I knelt down and put my hands on the surface, letting my senses discover as much as possible about the sudden change. As far as I could tell, the entire bay was now covered by a smooth, featureless single mass of material that was holding the boat fast.

This was why nothing else had been trying to stop them from leaving.

Holding my palms just above the surface, I tried to push a hole through it as I had before in the chamber. This time, however, there was no movement, even when I tried to draw as much power as I was able to from the Sun Heart. I gave up after a few attempts, feeling exhausted. This was not the same as the walls of the chamber. This was one, solid structure; seamless, contourless and entirely indivisible. I could only break it up by destroying everything from the furthest edge of the bay to the chamber itself. I had no idea how to generate such a force or what the consequences would be even if I could.

I hung my head, then looked back in the direction of the chamber. "This is not finished yet," I said, knowing that my words would be heard by the creature inside.

I quickly got to my feet and ran to the ship. As I got to the ladder at the stern, I met McCallan, Ferguson and a couple of the other men climbing down with a variety of boat hooks, axes and picks. They seemed startled to meet me and looked at me and the Sun Heart suspended in the air with a degree of apprehension, before hurrying past to the front of the boat.

I watched them for a few moments, then climbed the ladder and walked round the main cabin to the stairs leading to the bridge. I ran up them and opened the door at the top.

"Tell them to turn the engines off, Captain," I said as I walked inside.

"Turn them off?" the captain asked. "How are we going to get out of here otherwise?"

"We can't use them at the moment and we're only wasting fuel."

The captain paused.

"If you don't believe me, take a look at the men you sent out to break up the ice holding the boat. You'll find that they won't even be able to scratch the surface."

The captain left the bridge and I watched him as he made his way to the front of the boat and shouted down to the men below. He stayed there for a minute or so before walking slowly back up to the bridge.

When he got back inside, he looked at me and the Sun Heart with something close to contempt. It was clear that he not only blamed me for the current situation, but also that he didn't know what to do about it. The frustration of not being in control was written in every line of his face.

Without saying anything to me, the captain spoke down the tube to the engine room beneath. A few moments later the engines were silent and an eerie calm settled over the bay. On the deck, the men all looked up at the bridge with surprise.

The captain looked at me. "So how are you going to get us out of here?" he asked with mounting impatience. "We're all waiting."

"I'm not entirely sure at the moment."

The captain clenched his fists tightly and slammed one down onto the console next to the wheel.

"You're not sure?" he shouted. "When are you going to give up?"

"I'm not going to give up," I said sharply. "That's what it wants us to do."

"Maybe it's the only alternative," said the captain. He pointed back to the mountains. "That creature in the chamber has made its move and if you don't have one to answer it, you'll have to face up to the fact that you've lost."

"I didn't say I wasn't going to do anything. I just said that I wasn't sure how I was going to get us out of here."

The captain's mouth dropped open slightly and his eyes widened in disbelief. "This isn't a game, Alfred. I'm not playing with words here. I have ten men I'm responsible for and their lives are currently in your hands. What are you going to do?"

"Captain," I said, softening my tone. "You're just going

to have to trust me. It's not something that I fully understand. I'm still finding out what I'm capable of doing. I can sense and feel things that I know I shouldn't be able to feel, but at the same time it feels completely normal, like I've always been able to. I'm connected to everything. I can touch and feel everything. As I move my hand I can scrape the top of that mountain range. I can feel the texture of the rocks, the small pieces of moss clinging to them, the gaps in the stone. I can take a boulder from up there and bring it here as if I were picking a stone off the shore to skim in the sea."

The captain looked at me sceptically.

"I'll show you," I said.

I concentrated on a section of the highest peaks, feeling for a suitably sized piece of rock. We both watched as what started as a small speck in the distance quickly grew bigger and bigger until a large boulder came crashing down onto the solid surface covering the bay and carried on skidding directly towards the ship, coming to a halt a small way off.

"That's very impressive, Alfred," the captain said with more than a touch of impatience, "But you'll have to explain to me how moving rocks is going to help us here?"

"I'm no genius, Captain, but if we can't break the ice from around the ship we need to move the ship out of the ice."

"Can't you break this stuff like you did in the chamber?" asked the captain.

"No, I've already tried. This is different; this is a single piece of matter. As long as it remains like this I can do no more than McCallan out there with one of those boat hooks."

"So how are you going to move the ship out of the ice?"

"That's the bit I'm not sure about," I said, taking hold of the wheel and breathing in deeply to settle myself. "Are you ready, Captain?" I paused, waiting for the captain to respond, then added almost as an afterthought, "you'd better make sure those men get back on board."

The captain nodded and left the bridge.

Through the wood of the wheel and the console and the metal of the bridge, I felt along the sides of the ship, then down to the water beneath. The vessel was currently held completely immobile, the unbreakable ice on top of the bay moulding itself perfectly to every tiny deviation in the hull of the ship.

I closed my eyes and let my senses become flooded until the connections between everything became tangible and I could feel the infinitesimal separation between the hull and the ice, like the invisible gap between two magnets joined together.

As if I were easing fingers between this impossible divide, I gently separated the hull from the surface, cupping the vessel within my extended grasp.

As the ship started to become free, it wobbled slightly and the men on the deck reached out and grabbed hold of the top of the gunwales. With my eyes still closed, I pushed away from the surrounding ice. Very slowly, the ship started to rise, inching its way up, until it stood with its keel dripping a few feet above the surface, which had now completely closed underneath the boat.

I continued to push against the solid surface until the boat was a hundred feet in the air.

The men had been looking over the gunwales in shocked silence as they felt the boat lifting, but when they saw that it was clear from the grip of the ice they all let out a great cheer.

The captain came back on to the bridge, shocked and bewildered. "Are you making the ship fly, Alfred?"

"Don't sound so surprised, Captain," I said, opening my eyes again. "You've just been talking to a polar bear and dancing for someone not of this Earth. A flying ship should seem positively normal."

The captain said nothing. He was obviously not going to recognise my achievement in any way by asking how I had done this.

"Let's see if I can get us out to sea, shall we?" I said, breaking the silence.

I was controlling the height of the ship by keeping in contact with the surface, and I managed to slowly turn the vessel around by reaching out to the mountains on either side of us and altering the forces between them and the ship.

Then, keeping in contact with the mountainsides, I began to move forward as though I were placing my palms on the rockface of the cliffs, pulling us along one hand at a time.

I felt a shift in the surface below us and the boat started to slowly fall towards the ground. The solid mass that had previously provided the resistance to drive against had turned back to snow. Now there was only the real ice and water to push against. I managed to stop the ship falling, but it was much harder to control and to move forward at the same time.

The men had dropped to the ground when the ship started to fall, but now they stood up and gazed over the sides of the boat, watching the snow as it travelled with incredible speed towards the sea ahead of us.

"What's our host doing now?" the captain asked.

"I don't know," I said. "But I would suspect that the idea is to try and stop us from leaving."

"Well, can't you go any faster?" the captain said irritably.

"I'm sure that if I had enough practice, I could move much more quickly, but at the moment I'm very limited in what I can do. Let's just see if I can get out of here before the way is blocked."

The snow that had reached the opening was piling up between the two peaks on either side, great waves of white rolling over each other, building up and up into a solid, unbreakable barrier that would eventually completely fill the gap.

The captain looked at me. "Will you be able to fly over the top?" he asked.

"No. I've been trying to get us higher, but I can't do it," I replied.

"Why not?"

"We're in the air because I'm pushing away from the ice and water. As I move us further up I increase the force and the ice just gets pushed down into the bay. I'm sure there's another way of doing this, but I can't work it out at the moment."

"What are you going to do then?" demanded the captain.

I didn't say anything, but turning my head round, I took in all the tall, jagged and impossibly steep mountains encircling the bay. I saw the large dip in the rugged outline that was the only other way out of the bay, but quickly turned my attention back to the opening to the sea in front of us and continued to move the ship forward.

To the captain and to anyone looking at the scene it was as if I was driving the ship directly towards the ever-increasing wall of snow.

"What are you doing, Alfred?" asked the captain, a note of alarm entering his voice, as it became obvious that the ship was never going to make it over the obstruction. Again, I didn't respond and continued heading towards the giant wall that was still building in height and thickness.

"Alfred?" demanded the captain as we got closer.

I still said nothing. I looked back at the way we had come. Practically all of the snow was now in front of us. Only a small strip, like a life line, led back to the chamber in the mountainside and the creature within.

It was now or never, I thought.

"Captain, you have to trust me. Tell the men to hold on to something."

The captain stared into my eyes, trying to fathom what I was thinking.

"There's very little time," I said, as calmly as I could.

With obvious reluctance, the captain turned away from me and left the bridge. He stood on the platform outside the door and shouted down to the men at the front of the boat.

"Hold onto something!"

The men looked up, but no one moved, each face staring back at the captain with fear and confusion.

"Now! Damn you!" the captain shouted again, and everyone roused themselves from their shock and reached out for something to hold on to.

We were still at least half a mile away from the wall of ice, but the barrier towered over us, filling the sky, making us seem no more than a fly charging at an elephant.

The captain re-entered the bridge and I made sure that he and everyone on deck had grabbed hold of something. Then I turned the ship completely around so that we faced in the opposite direction and headed straight towards the gap in the mountain range on the other side of the bay.

The captain stared at me in surprise and was about to say something when a sound like a hundred explosions detonated and echoed across the bay.

Everyone looked back to see the wall of snow breaking up and an avalanche the size of a mountain heading towards us far quicker than we were travelling away from it.

I increased our speed as much as I could, reaching out time and again, further and further, to try and pull us along faster. But we could still feel the air rushing past us from behind, pushed forward by the wall of snow that was quickly catching up with us; a dire messenger of what was to come.

The men stared back in horror at the advancing mass of snow, now only hundreds of feet behind us.

In desperation I reached out as far as I could see, right up to the tops of the mountains on either side of the pass. I felt the connections to the peaks and wrapped my extended senses over the rocks like the hands of a giant, pulling with all the force I could muster from the Sun Heart.

But I was using too much force over too small an area. Whole sections of rock erupted from the summits and the boat suddenly began to judder and slow down.

I forced myself to relax and not think about what was approaching us. I was in a battle again. I needed to concentrate on the task I had to do and forget everything else. That's what I had been trained to do. All other sights and sounds faded away. I knew the captain was shouting, but his voice came to me as no more than a whisper.

I reached out again, gathering more of the mountain tops into my grasp and drawing power in increasing amounts from the Sun Heart rather than all at one time.

The avalanche of snow was only inches from our stern. We started to accelerate, faster and faster, moving through the air with dizzying speeds and covering the last few miles to the shoreline at the edge of the bay in a matter of seconds. We had far outpaced the advancing snow and I looked back to see the entire mass collapse onto itself as it gave up the chase.

I slowed the boat down as we approached the steep rise to the top of the pass and turned to speak to the captain. Before I could say anything I felt the boat lurch and lose speed, as if it had snagged on something in the water.

But we were a hundred feet up in the air.

Chapter 27
Over the Mountain

"What is it now?" asked the captain.

"It's the creature, Captain," I said. "It can't stop us with the snow, so it's trying to pull us back."

"Pull us back?"

"Yes."

"If it can do this, why didn't it do it earlier?"

"I don't know." It was a good question and it made me wonder. "I can sense the power of the creature's ship, and it's impossible for the creature to succeed with everything that I have at my disposal from the Sun Heart."

"What's it doing then?"

"It underestimated me in the chamber and it underestimated me when we got to the ship. I don't think it expected me to be able to control the Sun Heart, let alone to get this far. It knows it's been defeated and it's almost begging me to return the Sun Heart."

"Maybe you should give it back. It's not yours, Alfred. It's not even of this world; who knows what will happen if you take it away from here."

I ignored the captain's remarks and as though I was tearing a page from a book, I released us from the grip of the creature, allowing the ship to continue to the top of the pass unhindered.

"You're right. We don't know what will happen. But I would rather have this than give it back to a creature whose intentions we have even less chance of understanding."

The captain showed little sign of being convinced.

"You have no idea how powerful the Sun Heart is," I continued. "I've only used a tiny fraction of its capabilities. If I can learn to control it, there's no limit to what it can do. Think about it. We have both survived unimaginable horrors, inflicted on us and millions of other people by a small number of tyrannical men. These dictators could never win against the power of the Sun Heart. This could be used to stop wars. It could change our world."

"All hail, King Alfred," the captain scoffed. "But really, you're just guessing, aren't you? You have no idea what it is or what it can do."

"This is too important to ignore; to give back. The Sun Heart chose me for some reason."

"It chose you?"

"Yes, Captain. This is what saved me from the *Stanford*."

"How could it have saved you?"

"I don't know how, but it did. I remember everything now. How else could I have survived? The Sun Heart pulled me out of the sinking ship when otherwise I would have just been one more of the many who didn't stand a chance. And it's helping me now; it's guiding me. It wants me to take it away from here; I can feel it."

"It wants you to? Listen to what you're saying, Alfred. It's got a hold on you, just like it had a hold on us in the chamber." The ship crested the summit of the mountain pass and a completely new panorama opened up before us. The freshness of the sight made me realise how trapped I had felt by the struggle to leave the bay; it was like escaping into another world.

The mountain continued in long sweeping descents to the valley floor. On the other side of the valley, the next mountain range rose up gently until it peaked higher than our current position, blocking out any further view. To the left, the valley fanned out to meet the sea. The late afternoon sun shone from below the clouds and rays of golden light sparkled and shimmered on the shifting waves, leaping into the air as if applauding our arrival.

I turned to the captain with a smile of triumph.

"Look at what can be achieved, Captain. We're in a ship and we've just sailed over a mountain."

The captain seemed to have been similarly affected by the sudden sense of release the new landscape gave us. His tone lost some of its hardness. "I know, Alfred; it is incredible. Whatever I think of the rights and wrongs of it, you have achieved what you said you would."

I nodded, acknowledging the captain's words, then turned my attention to the way down the mountain.

The captain continued, his voice soft and full of wonder.

"That such a thing should exist; that such power can be given."

I looked back at the captain. He seemed different; there was a dream-like quality to the manner in which he was staring at the Sun Heart.

"Captain?" I asked, a little alarmed. "Are you all right?"

"Yes, Alfred, I'm fine, thank you," he said without taking his eyes from the Sun Heart. "It looks like it's just glowing, but at the same time it seems to be shining with a light bright enough to blind. How can it be so small and yet so powerful?"

The captain stretched out a hand towards the Sun Heart.

"Captain!" I shouted. I raised my hand from the wheel to ward off the captain as I had done before, but this time the captain stayed where he was, reaching out. I concentrated harder, trying to summon the power needed to move the captain away, but nothing was happening. "Captain, don't touch it," I warned and tried to push him backwards, but the captain brushed me away easily with his other arm and I watched helplessly as his large hand closed round the shining orb.

The light from the Sun Heart immediately died and, with a sickening lurch, the ship started falling through the air. I grabbed the wheel and the captain let go of the Sun Heart and reached forward to hold on to the edge of the console. We just had time to see the men at the front of the boat being thrown together and trying desperately to keep hold of anything before we were both thrown to the floor of the bridge by the impact of the ship hitting the ground and falling quickly over onto its side.

I ended up against the side of the bridge being pitched in all directions as the vessel careered down the mountain, gathering speed. I heard the alternate sounds as the ship scraped over the rocks and then slid over the snow, and the silences when we left the ground for a second or two as the ship hurtled off ledges and outcrops before smashing down again. Then the tortured sound of metal increased tenfold from all directions, quickly followed by the almost explosive noise of the ship stopping abruptly against something massive and hard.

There was the sound of rocks falling on the ship as I struggled to move from where I had ended up.

"Captain!" I called out weakly. "Are you there?"

There was no answer and I could see no trace of him in the dim light on the bridge. I had to assume he had been thrown out of a window by the initial impact.

I tried to shift my legs so that I could stand up, but one of them screamed with pain. I started slowly crawling up the sloping floor of the bridge using my good leg to push against anything that I could find. I felt something by my stomach; reaching down, I pulled up the Sun Heart from where it had come to rest against my body.

I held it in front of me with both hands. "You must help me now. Please!" I shouted at it, shaking it. "You must come back and take me from here." But nothing happened. No light emerged and there was no change in the dull grey surface of the object.

I could still hear rocks falling onto the boat; I had to get out if I was able. I pushed myself up towards the door leading out of the bridge to the cabin below, my hands still holding the Sun Heart in front of me.

Part 5: Endings and Legends
Chapter 28
Watching the Moon

The noise of rocks smashing into the ship stopped abruptly. The contorted metal of the crushed bridge vanished from around me. I wasn't crawling anymore and was no longer holding the Sun Heart.

I looked around my bedroom in confusion.

"What happened?" I stammered. "Where's the ship? I was just making my way out of the bridge."

Uncle Digit, sitting opposite me at my table, waited patiently for me to recover myself. "I didn't want you to see anymore, Finn," he said gently. "So I pulled us all the way out, back to your room. Alfred didn't get any further. That was where I found him forty years later."

I sat, quietly thinking about everything I had experienced. In one sense I had been away for months, living Alfred's life day to day from the time he left home, but I knew that in real time, it had been much shorter. I looked at my watch.

"It's only been four minutes," I said absentmindedly.

Uncle Digit was concentrating on his own thoughts and didn't say anything, so I remained silent as well. Eventually, he raised his hand up slowly and folded his fingers around the Sun Heart. The light went out and he lowered his hand and the

Sun Heart to the table.

He looked at me. I could see he was struggling with something.

"What are you thinking?" I asked.

"I've watched parts of my father's journey a number of times, but there are some things I still don't fully understand."

"What do you mean?"

"I'm not entirely sure. It just doesn't feel right." He paused, his eyes focused beyond me as he worked through his thoughts. He must have come to some decision, because his face relaxed and he looked at me again like someone who had moved out of the shadows. "But I tell you what, Dear Boy; when I get back I will have the whole thing sorted out."

He stood up, putting the Sun Heart in his pocket. I suddenly remembered that this wasn't the end of it; that he was going to return to goodness knows what.

"Back? Do you really have to?" I asked. "You have the Sun Heart. Couldn't you just keep it?"

He looked down at me and smiled. "It didn't seem to be the best course of action for my father, did it? And to tell you the truth, I'm beginning to feel that I don't have an option."

"What do you mean?" I asked.

"For one thing, keeping something this powerful and dangerous isn't a very good idea. But apart from that, Dark Star has been inside my head and I can't be a hundred percent certain that I managed to hide everything about sending the

Sun Heart here, to you. I couldn't have Dark Star coming looking for it now, could I?"

I had to admit that I wasn't very keen on the idea. "But you're not going to leave straight away?"

"No, I think the world is safe for a few more days." He laughed, and I laughed with him. For a moment I forgot that his words had some truth in them; forgot that there were beings from another world fighting over this one; forgot that he'd become part of this battle. I just enjoyed being with someone who had always managed to make me smile and laugh, even in my darkest moments.

The days were soon over, though. Uncle Digit and I were in my room discussing anything other than Sun Hearts, aliens and talking bears. But I knew it couldn't last and, after a small pause in our conversation, Uncle Digit stood up.

"Okay, Finn, it's time for me to say my goodbyes. Shall we go downstairs?"

My stomach turned to lead, but I tried to stay calm. "Okay," I said.

"You won't go troubling your mother with any stories about impossible things happening and the world ending, will you?" he said, reaching to take my crutches from beside the bed.

"No, I won't. But you have to promise that you'll come back here straight away?"

He leant down and kissed my forehead. "It's a deal," he

said, handing me my crutches.

I stood up and we shook hands on it. I tried to answer his cheerful smile with one of my own, but it was too hard and I felt a tear slowly roll down my cheek. Uncle Digit gently wiped it away. "Don't worry, Champ," he said, trying to sound reassuring. "I'll be back before you know it."

We went downstairs and Mum and I stood by the gate watching as he walked down the hill into town. He turned round to wave every so often until he was out of sight.

"Doesn't he have a bag or something?" Mum asked, waving back, a note of despair in her voice.

"I think he gets everything he needs on the way," I answered sheepishly; it wasn't exactly a lie, after all.

And then I had to wait, counting the hours and days until either he came back or ... or what? What if Uncle Digit lost? I remembered him telling me all the ways in which Dark Star could destroy the planet.

As the days moved on, I started looking at the moon every evening, wondering if it was getting any larger.

One day it appeared low on the horizon, looking as big and bright as the sun.

"Is that normal?" I asked Mum, trying to sound casual.

"I think so," she replied. "The moon always looks bigger when it's low down in the sky. It's beautiful, isn't it?"

"Yes, it is," I replied. "From a distance."

Mum gave me an odd look.

More days passed. I was going down the hall to the kitchen, wondering just how long it would take Uncle Digit with his new powers to get to the Arctic Circle and back when the phone rang. I leant against the wall and picked up the receiver.

"Hello?" I said tersely. There was no reply and there seemed to be a lot of static on the line. I was about to put the receiver back when I heard a crackly voice say, "Hello, Finn."

I nearly fell over with excitement. "You're okay?" I said, a little scream coming out.

"Yes, of course I am." I heard him laughing. "Did you ever doubt it?"

"No, of course not," I lied. "What happened?"

"I'll tell you all about it when I get back. I was just ringing so you know that everything's okay. I'll be back to see you in a few days. Can you wait till then?"

"No!" I shouted.

"That's the spirit. See you soon. Bye."

"Bye," I said, replacing the phone and putting my head against the wall to stop myself from falling over again.

The next few days were the slowest of my life. I spent most of my spare time looking out of the window and constantly asking Mum if she'd heard anything yet.

Then Mum was pushing me up the hill on the way back from school and she just said, "well, hopefully this will cheer you up." I had been lost in thought and wasn't sure what she'd said. I lifted my head and saw Uncle Digit leaning against our gatepost, smiling at me. He straightened up as he saw me and walked down to meet us.

"Hello, Finn," he said, rubbing my head thoroughly before giving Mum a kiss on the cheek. "Hello, sis. It's good to see you." He took the wheelchair from her and pushed me the remainder of the way to the house. I was bubbling with excitement and full of questions I knew I couldn't ask yet.

"You're rather quiet," Mum said, unlocking the front door. "Don't you have anything to say to your uncle?"

"Yes, sure," I said hesitantly. "How are you?"

"I'm all in one piece, thank you," he replied, laughing softly.

"Well, that's an improvement at least," Mum said as she took her coat off and moved out of the way so that the wheelchair could be pushed through the hall. "Now, I know you want to be with your uncle, but you also need to do your homework and I think Uncle Henry needs to rest after his journey, so we'll all go and sit in the kitchen. I'll make a pot of tea and you can finish your schoolwork."

We had our tea and Uncle Digit chatted with Mum. Sometimes he would smile and wink at me as if to say 'not long now, Dear Boy'.

Eventually, homework and supper were finished. Mum said, "Off you go. Clean your teeth and get ready for bed, and maybe your uncle will come and tell you a story."

I looked at him expectantly.

"I'm sure I can come up with something," he said, a broad grin breaking out on his face.

I took my crutches, leaving the kitchen quickly, and bum-shuffled my way upstairs. A few minutes later I was in bed leaning up against my pillows. Uncle Digit came in and pulled up the chair to sit near me.

"You have to tell me everything," I demanded.

"I promise I won't leave anything out," he replied.

And this is what he told me.

Chapter 29
The Forest

A week after leaving you and your mum, I was back in the logging town.

I didn't want to return to the research station. I had no need for food. I had no need for a bed. I just needed to be on my own, to try and work out what I was going to do.

I walked to the edge of the town and looked north into the endless swathes of forests stretched out in front of me. I walked forward into the trees and started running as fast as I could, paying no attention to the whips and lashes of the branches that struck me as I sped through the thick foliage. I ran until it was dark and I was sure I had left all trace of civilisation behind.

I stopped in a clearing and sat on a fallen trunk, collecting my thoughts.

It was so quiet.

I held my breath and listened to the silence. It was like the stillness of space.

My eyes wandered slowly across the trees and down to the forest floor, littered with leaves, fir cones and the detritus of countless yearly cycles of growth and decay.

How was I going to defeat Dark Star?

I wasn't a tactician and I didn't know how to plan a battle.

I couldn't even play chess, yet I was somehow meant to defeat a creature whose age was counted in millions of years and who had been responsible for conquering or destroying entire worlds.

I asked The Keeper many questions before I left, including how Dark Star could be killed. This had made The Keeper flinch, as if the mere act of thinking about such an event caused pain and discomfort. The Keeper couldn't tell me how to do this, but said that I could ask questions not related to ending the life of Dark Star.

After a slightly unusual version of twenty questions, I discovered that the shells protecting The First, maintaining every aspect of their bodily functions, were not completely indestructible. Although they were capable of withstanding a great many things, they were susceptible to high levels of pressure. When I asked what this limit was, or how to achieve the required level, The Keeper wouldn't say and told me that further information was in the Sun Heart.

The Keeper's thoughts were usually precise and there was very little doubt about their meaning. But here, The Keeper hadn't said that the Sun Heart would teach me, or that the Sun Heart would show me how to defeat Dark Star; the answer was vague and unclear.

Where would I look for this further information?

There was little I could do but travel back inside the Sun Heart, retracing my steps, retracing Alfred's steps, looking for anything that might help me.

I took out the Sun Heart and opened it, leaving it floating in the air an arm's length away, its soft glow almost unnoticed, like a trick of light glimpsed in the corner of the eye.

Once more I swam through the black, star-filled skies of the Crystal World, following The First on their pilgrimage around the Crystal Lake and re-exploring the worlds inside the world that was the Citadel.

Days, if not weeks, passed as I searched for guidance through the great wealth of history and knowledge that was available to me.

I carefully re-examined everything that my father had been able to achieve with the Sun Heart. He could push objects away from him or shield himself to stop them from coming any closer. He could extend his senses to feel all the way to the bottom of the crater, pull boulders from the tops of the mountains and lift a ship clear from the water and move it through the air.

I closed the Sun Heart and dropped my head, staring at the ground in despair.

How had Alfred been able to accomplish so much, so easily?

I could do none of these things.

So far, I had only travelled inside the Sun Heart; I had never tried to use its power to achieve anything out here, in the real world.

Inside the Sun Heart, there was no sensation of existing in the world outside. Somehow, I needed to connect to the Sun Heart while remaining conscious of everything here in the outside.

I opened the Sun Heart again. The gentle, invitational breeze it gave out brushed my face and I stared ahead of me, trying to relax and think about what I was going to do.

Instead of falling into the space I called the Waiting Room, as I had done so many times before, I imagined the Waiting Room falling into me, that I somehow contained the Sun Heart.

There was a blinding flash of light and I was hurled fifty feet through the air, smashing into a tree and falling back down to the ground. I lay for a minute collecting myself, then slowly got to my feet and walked back to where I had been sitting.

The Sun Heart was lying on the ground, inactive.

I picked it up, thinking that I probably shouldn't try to absorb all of the energy from a star in one go. The Sun Heart must have turned itself off as a safety mechanism, discharging the excess power.

My clothes were charred, but apart from that there was no damage.

I tried a few more times, with similar results, until I became aware that controlling the flow of power from the Sun Heart was similar to breathing.

I learnt to relax more and master this until I could feel the power ebb and flow within me like inhaling and exhaling air.

With the control of power, other things started happening.

I began to be able to sense things as my father had; I could feel my hands extending beyond my fingers, touching and moving things far from where I was.

I stood there, running my senses over the ground, then up among the trees, reaching out as far as I could see, right up to the snow taking flight in the wind on the top of the mountains.

Over the next few days, I learnt how to manage these new capabilities. I learnt how to spread my senses as far as possible, or to focus them on individual objects. To be able to discern each minute detail and every change in texture and even colour.

I could feel the very real difference between inanimate objects and living things, following the life flowing through the trees, moving from root to trunk to branch to leaf. I could sense the silent fear in animals hiding in the snow-covered undergrowth and the hunger and single-minded determination radiating from one of the hardy northern goshawks searching the ground for any tell-tale movement from her perch, high in the trees.

As I brushed past these lives, I felt them start, as if I had ruffled their fur or feathers with my fingers. This surprised me in turn. I wondered that if my clumsy attempts at reaching out could be detected, could I communicate with these creatures? Could I reach inside their minds and govern them in some way?

At first, any attempt I made to do more than skim my

senses over the goshawk made her fly away in alarm. But I followed her flight each time, stretching my senses as she moved around the forest avoiding me or carrying out her daily routines. In doing so, I learnt the rhythm of her life; the thrill of her soaring freedom, her solitary habits, her fears and desires. I adapted my contact to be in tune with her ways and her needs. Gradually I gained the trust of this shy creature enough that she would stay when I reached out to her, bound to me from afar as though she were strapped to my outstretched arm.

I wondered if I could control her more; if I could ask her to fly to me here in the clearing.

I stood up and held out my arm expectantly. I called to her; my thoughts flowing from me and connecting to hers, enticing her with visions of open skies and easy prey. But she remained on her branch far away, uncertain and fearful.

I called to her again and waited, my heart racing with anticipation and doubt, my senses straining to catch the slightest motion.

I wondered if I was asking too much, both of myself and of the bird. But then I sensed the rush of air as her wings' strong pulse lifted her from the branch and she dropped to glide effortlessly through the forest, adjusting her flight with small deft movements to avoid anything in her path.

She burst through the trees to my right, not much higher than the ground, and headed straight towards me, only fully opening her broad wings at the last moment to brake and rise and land on my arm with a grace that took my breath away.

She folded her wings and gave me a quick look with what I couldn't help thinking were eyes full of surprise, then turned away to look around her, padding her talons on my arm as if not sure whether to stay or take flight again. I calmed her, reassuring her that the skies were still hers to command and that she was free to roam where she would. I told her that she would not want for food and showed her where the maimed and the old animals lay that would not survive this winter.

She looked at me again, then turned her head back, eyes focused on where I had indicated. She stayed still for a minute then stiffened slightly as she spotted movement before launching herself from my arm and floating in complete silence towards the undergrowth. There was a brief scuffle before she re-emerged with a small animal clutched between her claws. She landed on the trunk a few feet away and held on to the animal tightly with one claw until it had stopped moving.

I watched her eat, captivated by her beauty and presence. She didn't have a name, so I called her Grace and she took the name, flying back to guard her range above the trees. But she stayed close and when I heard her sharp cry the next day, I showed her where to hunt and called her to me from time to time.

In the same way I began to understand all the creatures that lived around me in the forest and how to lull them with the lilting songs of their lives until I could command them almost instantly.

I didn't spend all of my time with the animals. I also learnt how to move objects, adjusting the power I needed to the size of the object or the distance and speed I wanted it to travel. I learnt how to create a shield, either around myself or around other objects, that was strong enough to withstand the force of anything I could throw against it.

And I discovered how to fly!

It wasn't flying in the true sense. I pulled myself towards objects, hurtling along the ground or through the air towards anything I could see. It was painful at first, until I worked out how to stop myself from crashing into things by pushing away from them, but soon I was able to take to the skies with Grace, wheeling and diving alongside her as she soared and swooped, skimming the tops of trees, screaming at the top of my voice.

But even though I was continually amazed at what I could now do, I knew that I only understood a tiny fraction of the capabilities of the Sun Heart; that The Keeper and Dark Star could wield the full power of this incredible device without thinking, in the same way as we use our bodies, as if everything were just part of themselves to do with and command as they saw fit.

I could have stayed in the forest trying to master the Sun Heart for years and I still wouldn't have been certain that I had learnt enough to defeat Dark Star. But in the time I had spent, I had managed to draw a plan together, thread by thread, until it felt as though I at least had some idea of what to do; that there was a small ray of light to guide me through the darkness of the task I had in front of me.

And I knew it was time to leave.

Chapter 30
How to Recruit an Army

I said goodbye to Grace and made my way north.

Now that I could fly, I covered the huge distance back to the bay in a matter of hours. I approached the great circle of mountains surrounding the bay and slowed down, a slight sinking feeling souring the excitement of the journey.

Flying along the lower slopes of the western range, I hugged the mountains until they started turning round on the northern side, then turned in and flew up the steep jagged sides, landing in the snow near the top of the low point between two peaks, hoping to arrive close to the giant snow columns that marked out The Keeper's domain.

The Sun Heart had been my constant light, staying the same distance in front of me as I flew, like a beacon guiding me forwards. I closed it now and stood in the snow, listening.

A cracking sound was coming from inside the bay, like someone smashing rocks. Then there was nothing. Then I heard another crack, then a longer silence, then again, another crack.

I scrambled through the snow with more urgency, wondering what this was. The snow flattened out at the top and I dropped to my stomach, crawling forward to look down into the bay.

I could see The Keeper's columned structure, almost dead

ahead on the northern flanks of the mountains. About half into the bay from the columns, a mass of a hundred or so birds flew around in circles; seagulls, terns and other Arctic birds, each one robbed of its own colours, transformed into the uniform blackness that was the marque of Dark Star.

Below this living tornado of feathers there were about ten bears, equally unnatural in their blackness, ranged in a line, with Dark Star's malign presence on the platform in the middle of everything.

The animals were silent. The cracking was the sound of large boulders smashing into The Keeper's dwelling from time to time. There was no sign of The Keeper, or of the bears and the fox; I presumed that they were all inside the structure.

As I watched this all-too-strange spectacle, I heard a high-pitched call and looked up to see a couple of Arctic terns flying overhead. Their path was taking them to the left of Dark Star, but as they flew further into the bay, they veered towards the black throng of whirling birds. They called out louder and strived against the force pulling them, their wings beating frantically to drive them back on their course. But the struggle was over quickly; soon the black of their caps flowed down along the sleek lines of their body, until all of their pure white feathers became uniformly dark and they vanished into the multitude of birds flying around in endless circles above Dark Star.

I stayed where I was for an hour at least, studying Dark

Star's actions and trying to grasp what was happening.

The attacks were coming from all directions, every two to five minutes. Although I knew that Dark Star was controlling them, it was as though there were hundreds of powerful catapults positioned all around the bay, launching enormous rocks with trajectories perfectly calculated so that wherever they originated from they all landed exactly on that one, single target.

By the time these huge slabs and boulders crashed into the towering columns they were travelling with considerable speed. Most of them broke apart on impact, the pieces falling to the ground where they mysteriously rolled slowly away from the columns for a few hundred yards, as if blown along by the breath of a giant.

It was strange to watch this very ancient form of siege warfare being practised by the most technically advanced people in the galaxy. At first I thought that Dark Star might be acting out of frustration and boredom, but this seemed unlikely; I realised that there must have been a reason behind the behaviour.

I wondered how long this had been going on. I knew that The Keeper's power source had been heavily depleted after Dark Star first arrived. Keeping up any kind of defence against this continuous barrage would eat into what reserves were left, weakening them little by little until eventually they collapsed.

So I guessed that this colossal skittles match was a waiting game: at some point I would come back to return the Sun Heart and Dark Star wanted to reduce whatever resources The Keeper had that would help me.

Whatever abilities my new skills gave me, I was less than certain that I could fight or defend against all of these and still carry out what I needed to do to defeat Dark Star, even with The Keeper's help. I had no idea how weakened The Keeper was and I needed something to balance out the advantage that these creatures gave to Dark Star.

I needed my own army.

Moving down the mountain a safe distance, I opened the Sun Heart and flew back to the lower slopes.

I had never tried to reach out so far before, but I stretched my senses all the way I had come, all the way back through the snow and the mountains and the forests, all the way to the clearing and to Grace, sheltering from the cold wind in the branches of the tall white pines.

I told her that I needed her, that I needed her and many other goshawks, that she was going to help me defeat something powerful enough to destroy her world, something that could take her freedom, something that could fold up the sky and stop her wings from unfurling.

I felt her assent and I knew that she would come to me, even across the thousands of miles of frozen wilderness. But I needed her to lead the others that I would find, who would trust me less.

Goshawks have large ranges and can be spread out over a vast area, but I found eighteen other birds that could fly to Grace within a day. One by one I called them to the clearing. I provided food for them and talked to them as they feasted. I reassured them that they would not be on their own, that they would be saving the wild openness of their skies and that I would protect them.

I waited until they had all eaten and were fully rested, then I commanded them to leave and they opened their great wings and ascended through the trees into a night sky bright with stars.

I would have at least four days before they reached me. In that time I needed to recruit whatever other creatures I could find in the vicinity.

I thought that if Dark Star had managed to ensnare a number of bears, I could also find some and tempt them away from their dens in the mountains here and beyond. Winter was approaching and the bears would be starting to dig their dens and curl up for months in a state of semi-hibernation. I searched the hillsides of the mountains that ringed the great crater, then, staying close to the shoreline, I searched the mountain ranges along the coast and the snow-covered tundra that lay between the mountains and the sea. Wherever I found anything living I would listen to their dreams, learning what I could of their ways and habits.

I found nothing useful in the short snuffling dreams of

the smaller animals, but the bears had expansive dreams full of imagery and colour. As I tentatively touched the minds of these sleeping giants, I discovered that The Keeper was known to all the bears as the Sun Spirit and had existed here from the time memories began. I was surprised to learn that Wind Over Mountain and Wind Over Sea had been venerated for countless generations as the Guardians of the Spirit.

I tried not to think of what it might mean for them to be trapped for centuries within the confines of the bay, their cubs never growing any older, their days repeating themselves through the seasons.

But with this knowledge I stole into the bears' dreams and roused them from their slumber, whispering to them as they awoke.

You must rise up. The Guardians, Wind Over Mountain and Wind Over Sea, are in danger and need your help. If you do not come now to fight, the Guardians will be defeated and the Sun Spirit will be lost for ever.

Shaking off the sleep of their winter dream-world, they stirred slowly and left the warmth of their dens, standing in the cold, uncertain why they were awake.

Eat to build up your strength, I told them, and they walked to the ocean to gorge on the prey I found for them before making their way to me at the foot of the crater mountains.

The first to reach me was a young female. She was

confused and suspicious when she saw that it was a human who had called her here. She circled me warily, sniffing the air all the time and growling in a manner to which I had become very accustomed.

I searched in her mind and found her name.

Greetings, Snow Dancing In Wind, I said to her. *You are not alone. Other bears are coming.*

She still looked at me with distrust and showed no sign of wanting to communicate with me, but she stopped circling and moved a small way off, lying down on an outcrop of rock, waiting to see if other bears would indeed turn up.

The other bears arrived one at a time over the next two days. When they were all with me I had six bears, all with names that I'm sure the fox would have remarked upon. As well as Snow Dancing in Wind, there was Water Flowing Over Ice, Lightning Striking Rock, Shadow In Moonlight, Rolling Thunder and Stars Moving On Waves.

These bears had not been altered by The Keeper. They were natural bears and were not able to speak in the manner that Wind Over Mountain and Wind Over Sea were able to. They were also not able to understand me when I was talking. As with all the other animals, the Sun Heart allowed me to enter the minds of these creatures, communicating in thoughts and images, and to be able to understand what they were thinking and feeling.

At that moment I was left in no doubt that they were not

there because of me, but for the Sun Spirit and for the Guardians of the Spirit.

Lightning Striking Rock lumbered towards me until he was only a few feet away. He was by far the largest of the bears, barely having to raise his head to look me in the eyes. There was a large scar running down his left cheek, made by a blow that would have blinded him if it had been a fraction higher. It was apparent that he was the leader and had been chosen to speak for all the bears.

Why do you hold the Light of the Sun Spirit? he asked. I knew that he would try to take the Sun Heart from me if he didn't like my answer.

The Light has been entrusted to me by the Sun Spirit, I told him.

The mistrust in his eyes hardened.

A Dark Spirit has arrived, I said. *An enemy of the Sun Spirit, who has vowed to steal the Light and to destroy our world.*

The bear's face broke out into a sneer, exposing teeth clearly capable of ripping off a man's arm.

The Sun Spirit and the Guardians have been here since there have been bears to remember, he said simply. *There is nothing that can overcome them. What you say is not possible.*

It was clear that I needed to do more to persuade this bear. I let some of my memories flow into the bear's mind, showing him what had happened to me since coming to the bay; my struggle with Dark Star and my meeting with The Keeper and all that was spoken between us.

When I had finished, Lightning Striking Rock said nothing, but his silence was one of disbelief and shock.

You heard the words of the Sun Spirit, I said. *The Sun Spirit fears that Dark Star will destroy this world. Dark Star cannot be defeated by the Sun Spirit, so the Sun Spirit has given the Light to me so that I might use its power to defeat Dark Star.*

The bear looked at me without saying anything for a full minute, his mind a mixture of thoughts I was unable to interpret.

I will speak with the others, he said eventually. *I will tell them what you have shown me and we will decide what must be done.*

He turned and re-joined the group of bears, while I sat down and waited.

After what felt like a very long time, Lightning Striking Rock walked back towards me. I stood up as he approached and stopped a little further from me than he had done before. I could sense his thoughts clearly now.

We understand now why the Sun Spirit has entrusted you with the Light. The being that you call Dark Star is known to us as the Night Spirit, he said. *All bears know that the Night cannot be defeated by the Sun, but can only be held back for

266

part of each day until the Time of Darkness, when all things end. That time has not yet come and you must send the Night Spirit back into the bottomless depths, to wait until the Time of Darkness comes.

So, you will help me? I asked.

We will help you defeat the Night Spirit, replied Lightning Striking Rock.

Thank you.

I was relieved, but I was also struck by the simple beauty of beliefs that held those most fundamental of truths at their heart and I hoped I would have the time to learn more about these.

The other bears had by now joined us and they were all standing nearby, looking at me expectantly.

There is something else I need to show you, I said hesitantly.

I allowed them to see what was currently taking place in the bay, a little fearful of how they would respond to seeing so many of their kind enslaved by Dark Star. After I had finished showing them everything, the bears remained silent, each one seemingly lost in their own thoughts.

Then Lightning Striking Rock looked up, his eyes filled with the weight of sadness of all the bears.

Do you know any of those bears? I asked him gently.

We have recently lost six bears, but I saw only four of them there.

I was having difficulty understanding his thoughts clearly as there were so many emotions swirling around.

To see any bear reduced to such an existence is a pain beyond all endurance, I managed to make out eventually. *Now, they are no longer bears and we will sing of their passing in time.*

He let out a sigh and shook himself slightly, as if throwing off a great coat of sorrows. *But now, we have a task to do,* he said, turning towards the mountainside and striding forward.

Hold on, I said running to catch up with him. *We have to wait a bit longer.*

If we need to act, we act now, he said.

Some more animals are coming to help us. We need them as well. This is not something we can do on our own.

He stared at me and then looked around at the other bears.

Very well, he said. *We will wait.*

One by one, the bears sat down, some of them lying down with their heads resting on their front legs, waiting patiently for whatever was going to happen next. I sat down with them as well and waited.

I remembered that my father had dreamt about doing this. He had dreamt about sitting down with the bears and discussing the stars.

Tell me about the stars, I said. *Do you have stories about them?*

Stories? said Lightning Striking Rock, making a small

guttural sound of dismissal. I waited to see if he was going to add anything, but he didn't seem to want to talk further. I looked at the other bears expectantly.

Water Flowing Over Ice raised her head.

You cannot make up stories about such things, she began. *There are only the Great Truths, handed down through the generations from the time of the First Great Bear.*

The First Great Bear?

Yes. You are not a bear, these are things you can never understand.

I would very much like to try.

Water Flowing Over Ice considered this and sat up.

You want to know how the stars began? she asked.

Yes, I do.

Very well. Long ago, the First Great Bear walked freely over the warm lands, basking in the sun, smelling the trees and the grass and the flowers, fishing in the rivers and the seas. But the Ice Spirit could not enjoy these things and was jealous. The Ice Spirit wanted to make the world a land of perpetual ice and cold, where nothing could grow and nothing could live. Many battles were fought between the First Bear and the Ice Spirit, battles lasting longer than the lifetimes of bears, battles that only ended when the First Bear destroyed the Ice Spirit with one mighty blow, shattering it into numberless crystals that flew into the sky beyond the sun, only to be seen at night, shining as a warning to all bears. For it is known that the stars move and speak to each other, planning for the time when they can join together, to become the Ice Spirit once more and take revenge against all life.

I gazed up at the billions of stars and galaxies.

And you're here to protect against that time? I suggested.

Yes. The First Great Bear took some snow and made the White Bears. He asked Mother Earth to breathe life into them and to protect them from the cold, for we are destined to walk only in the regions of snow and ice, guarding against the return of the Ice Spirit and keeping watch to ensure that the stars stay in the sky.

So, you cannot travel to the warm lands? I asked.

Not until the First Great Bear returns. Then we will know our work is done. Then we can leave the snow and ice and travel to the warm lands.

And so we sat and talked through the long star-filled night. I listened to their tales of the sea and the ice and of the beginning of all things until I sensed Grace's presence and looked up to see her and the other goshawks gliding through the moonlight towards us.

I stood up and watched as she swooped down and landed effortlessly on my outstretched arm while the other birds took perches on surrounding rocks. If the birds were nervous of the bears' presence, I couldn't detect this. Neither did the bears seem troubled by the arrival of the goshawks. I had kept in contact with Grace from time to time and had provided food at various points along their route. A little food was also available here, in the harsh snow-covered scrub along the mountain sides, and I showed them where this lay.

I waited until they had finished eating before explaining my rather simple plan to everyone.

I don't know if the animals under the control of the Night Spirit will be used to attack me or to attack the Sun Spirit. But these creatures must be engaged, bear against bear and bird against bird, to allow me to confront the Night Spirit alone. I will do whatever I can to protect you, but I cannot be certain I will be able to do this, or for how long.

We will do what is necessary, Lightning Striking Rock declared, making it clear that no such protection would be required by him.

We must rest now until morning, I said. *We will strike when it is light. As soon as the sun is up I will use the power of the Light to carry the bears to the top of the mountain ...*

I didn't get any further with my plan. The bears suddenly stood up and I could see their faces, lit by the reflected moonlight, staring at me in disbelief and horror. Lightning Striking Rock took a few threatening steps towards me.

No bear will be carried anywhere, he declared, the menace in his thoughts so tangible I could feel the hairs on the back of my neck stand up.

I took a deep breath. *How are we going to get into the bay?*

You are like a cub who doesn't know the way to the sea.

Yes, I sighed. *I think in some ways I am.*

Lightning Striking Rock took a step back and sat down again. *The Path of the Ancients has been used by bears to pass through the mountains since stories began,* he said.

The Path of the Ancients? Can this be reached by morning?

It is not far from here and can be reached in half of the current period of light.

I worked out that would be about two hours.

That still gives us time to rest. I will wake you before it is light.

Lightning Striking Rock said nothing else, but the bears returned to their positions and lay down.

The birds were not used to the temperatures this far north and were a bit restless standing on their rocky perches. I created a shield around all of us to keep out the wind and the cold and, as everyone slept, I ran over all of the events that had led to me being here, holding a device capable of destroying worlds and discussing battle tactics with six polar bears and a large number of goshawks. I had to keep my belief alive: the belief that what I was doing was the only option open to me and that I was capable of fulfilling everything that was required of me. These were not comfortable thoughts to carry me through the night. My main comfort lay in the fact that this time tomorrow it would all be over, one way or another.

Chapter 31

Battle

A few hours later, with the darkness still surrounding us, I removed the shield to wake everyone up and we headed into the mountains, following the bears.

The moon had set by now and the only light came from the myriad stars shining down in the flawless night sky.

As we walked up towards the high summits, I scoured the tops for something that looked like a pass, but couldn't see anything. The route we were taking headed towards an enormous flat bluff, towering thousands of feet straight up. This was the only variation in the otherwise unending series of jagged snow-covered peaks that created an impenetrable barrier into the bay. When we got closer, I saw that the vast block of stone had been split in two and there was a crack running down the entire length where the unimaginable forces that created the crater had riven this titanic piece of rock in two.

Is that the way to the Path of the Ancients? I asked the bears, pointing up to where I hoped the bears could see.

Lightning Striking Rock looked to where I was pointing. *It is,* he replied.

Grace and the other birds had already flown off into the mountains and I now left the bears as well and flew towards the pass, eager to see for myself where it came out.

I dropped down to the opening and peered inside. It was about twenty feet wide with the walls on each side continuing upwards almost completely sheer until they were blocked off, either by stone or by the ice and the snow. The glow from the Sun Heart barely penetrated the darkness and I wasn't sure how the bears managed to make their way across the rock-strewn floor in front of me, shimmering like mercury in my night vision.

It looked like a secret entrance to the underworld and I shivered as I lifted myself off the ground and flew slowly into the passage. I continued for a few hundred yards with one or two turns, before flying out of the passage into a cathedral-sized chamber, with walls glistening in the starlight that streamed down from the opening far above. I floated across this vast chimney in the mountains and entered a passageway on the other side. After another hundred yards, I came out into a much smaller cave, the roof and walls of which narrowed down to a small opening. I approached the opening cautiously and looked out into the bay.

Dark Star was about a mile away on the ice.

As I watched, another great boulder was launched from somewhere on the mountains towards The Keeper's snow pillars.

I turned back inside and called to Grace, letting her know where I was. A few minutes later the cave was full of wings and banking birds looking for suitable resting places in the semi-darkness. It was nearly dawn and I could sense that the bears hadn't arrived at the entrance to the pass yet. I turned to fly back down the passage just as the first rays of the sun rose from the water across the bay. The morning light shone directly into the cave, lighting up the inside with a warm glow and filtering down the passageway. I flew along the passage, back to the large chamber, marvelling as the light became amplified by the mineral deposits in the walls, bouncing back and forth, shining with an intensity many times greater than the light entering the chamber and flooding down the passageway that led to the opening on the other side of the mountain.

Here indeed was the Path of the Ancients.

Half an hour later the bears entered the chamber and a few minutes after that we were all assembled in the small cave.

I pointed down the side of the mountain to the snow pillars of The Keeper's stronghold.

You must make your way there and wait for the Sun Spirit and the Guardians of the Spirit to come out.

Lightning Striking Rock looked where I had pointed, then turned to me.

And what if they do not come? he asked.

If they do not come, we have lost, I said simply.

The bear looked back down.

Can we not be seen by the Night Spirit as soon as we step outside?

I will use the power of the Light to hide you as you descend. You will not be visible from the bay.

Staying inside the cave to ensure the Sun Heart could not be seen from outside, I extended my senses into the snow near the entrance, the Sun Heart allowing me to feel each tiny flake and every air gap between them. I pulled up a large section of the snow into a swirling flurry, as though it had been caught by a strong gust of wind, driving it like a small white tornado along the path that would be taken by the bears. As the snow settled back behind it, I fashioned a wall high enough for the bears to walk behind, but that looked little different from the snow that had been there before.

When it was finished, I turned to the bears.

It is safe for you to go now. I will let you know when it is time to join the battle, but it is important that you do not make your presence known before then.

Very well, said Lighting Striking Rock.

He led the other bears out of the cave and I watched as they walked down the mountainside and moved into position.

They wouldn't have long to wait, but first I needed something; something that my father had discovered forty years ago.

I closed my eyes and reached further out with my senses, as though I was crawling along on all fours, feeling my way down the mountain, down to the water's edge and under the snow and the ice to the sea. Down, down, following the steep shelving sides of the crater, searching down and still further down as my father had done, deeper and deeper, so deep that I thought I must be imagining how far I had gone. And there, right at the very end of everything, I found something so old, so ancient, that it had become a myth in the minds of those who travelled across the oceans, recounting and recreating stories that had once been part of the fabric of the seas. Here was the Kraken, the legendary devourer of ships and men from which even the great whales fled. I gently entered the mind of this ageless creature. Her name was Amara. Here she slept; the last of her kind, dreaming dreams of lives long past.

And so I awoke her.

Like the soughing of the wind in sails, I breathed life back into her with tales of times gone by, when she ruled the seas and all the oceans were her hunting grounds. I sang to her the song of the sea; a song of towering waves and waters teeming with life, a song of ships shrouded in mist and the cries of sailors calling to each other across the decks.

Slowly she stirred, searching for me. Why had her peace been disturbed? Why was she being woken?

Then I placed a fear in her heart, a fear that her peace would be taken away, that something more powerful than her was planning to destroy her forever, destroy her and everything else that was hers; that she would be gone and would not even be a memory in the sea foam washed to the shore by the tides.

I showed her The First, their history and their power. I

showed her Dark Star and Dark Star's desire for the end of all things. And I felt the fear inside her grow and I felt the desire to overcome this enemy grow. With these thoughts, I drew her slowly up from the darkness of the uncountable fathoms, whispering to her, telling her how she could defeat this threat to her peace and dreaming.

And as Amara began her long rise to the surface, I began my assault.

I had made no contact with The Keeper, certain that I would not be able to do this without also alerting Dark Star to my presence. I decided that the best way to let The Keeper know I was here was to strike at Dark Star.

Moving to the cave entrance I searched around for a suitably sized boulder, settling on one close by that was about the size of a house. I waited until Dark Star fired another rock towards The Keeper and then I launched my own, watching it shoot through the air like a small meteorite. Before it got to within a hundred yards of Dark Star, the rock suddenly changed course, flying back towards me like a well-struck baseball. I didn't move, but held both my hands out and guided the speeding boulder over my head, where it smashed into the side of the mountain above me.

A wave of pure hatred hit me; a giant roar of loathing and contempt emanating from Dark Star. I couldn't help smiling, knowing that it was me using the Sun Heart that had caused this; that for me to be wielding the power of The First would be seen as an unforgivable insult. This, rather than the boulder itself, was my first attack.

Dark Star's attention suddenly moved away from me. Looking down to my left, I saw The Keeper, the fox and four bears emerge from the entrance to the snow structure. I was surprised to see the extra bears and presumed that these were two of the six that Lightning Striking Rock had said had gone missing. The Keeper had saved these from the same fate as the ones that I now saw charging forward from their position on either side of Dark Star, leaving just the two bears that pulled the platform.

The birds above Dark Star had also broken from their constant circling, forming a wide flank three or four birds deep that streamed towards the five white figures.

I called to Grace, telling her to lead the goshawks and engage the birds. As they flew over my head from inside the cave I turned my attention to Lightning Striking Rock and the bears, calling them forward to protect The Keeper at all costs.

As the goshawks and the bears came into view I felt another mighty howl from Dark Star.

I intended to keep the advantage of surprise as long as I could, so I leapt from the cave mouth and quickly flew across the bay, landing in the snow halfway between Dark Star and the opening to the sea. This was near to the place where I had fallen through the last time I was here. It was the area in the bay where the ice was thinnest, and it was here that I needed to engage Dark Star if my plan were to succeed.

I stood up and waited, but Dark Star showed no intention of moving any closer to me. The anger and hatred I had felt before had changed into something approaching curiosity.

I felt a force pulling me slowly forwards, dragging my feet through the snow. I pushed against this, moving myself back to where I had been. The force increased, pulling me closer and I increased mine to match, moving myself back again. This carried on to the point where I could balance any level of force that Dark Star applied. Then the force stopped abruptly and I was swatted backwards towards the sea. It was almost a dismissive gesture, as if to say that the test was over and now the real work was going to begin.

I flew back to my position in time to see hundreds of boulders rising up from the mountains on every side of the bay. They were flying straight towards me. I managed to knock a few of them off course, but there were far too many for me, so I quickly created a shield around myself and the Sun Heart. I watched as the giant rocks hurtled towards me, raining down for at least a minute, completely covering the shield, until the only light was the glow from the Sun Heart.

The shield was holding, but I couldn't move the rocks and I wondered if Dark Star wanted to imprison me while his forces finished off The Keeper and our little army. The frustration of not being able to do anything started to make me panic. I had to stop all thoughts of failure and work out what to do. I had been afraid to draw too much power from the Sun Heart, as I knew that this could end up with the Sun Heart turning itself off. I needed to draw power from the Sun Heart directly into the shield, expanding this little by little until there was sufficient force to push the stones off.

At first, nothing seemed to be happening and the shield just absorbed the extra power, but then I started to hear small movements, then more and more until all at once there was an immense surge. All the heaviness fell from the rocks and it felt as though I was holding hundreds of juggling balls above my head.

In the time it had taken me to free myself, the black bears had drawn Dark Star to within a hundred yards of me. I heaved all of the rocks straight towards the platform, but instead of sending the rocks back to me, Dark Star swept all of them towards The Keeper and the battling bears, not caring if they would strike white or dark creatures. I saw animals of both hues turning and leaping out of the way of the rocks speeding in their direction. I was trying to make out through the tangled mass of rocks and animals whether The Keeper had been able to provide any protection, when I heard Grace calling me and looked up to see her being mobbed by a large number of birds.

Although the goshawks were far more manoeuvrable than the other birds and could avoid most attacks, Grace was struggling against so many birds and was desperately trying to evade all of the talons and beaks that were being aimed at her. I quickly threw a protective shield around her and saw two or three birds hurtle head-on into the shield and fall to the ground. I managed to pluck a few others and hurl them, cartwheeling through the air into the side of the mountains.

This didn't go unnoticed by Dark Star and I saw all of the birds suddenly leave whatever animal they had been attacking and make a line straight for Grace, who was taking whatever evasive actions she was able to. The other Goshawks were doing their best to fly in and out of the mass, knocking the occasional bird out of the sky, but I had to keep a shield around Grace at all times to protect her. This limited what I could do against Dark Star, who was now drawing me ever closer to tendrils that were glowing red with the heat of a blast furnace.

I was still pushing against Dark Star, trying to move back into position, but I was now close enough for the tendrils to strike and Dark Star began to rain blow upon blow onto my shield in a ceaseless tirade.

As well as protecting myself and Grace I was also trying to push Dark Star back to keep myself as far as possible from the tendrils. But in all of this, Dark Star had not seen any real attack coming from me. If I had to guess at any emotion that was coming from the swirling black cloud that was attacking me, I would say that my actions were causing amusement. A human face would have shown the grim, wry smile of someone sure of their superiority and the inevitability of their victory.

Dark Star suddenly started to push me down into the snow

with a force far stronger than had been used before. I struggled to oppose this and to protect myself from the continuous onslaught at the same time. I had the power of a sun to draw from; Dark Star only had the power of a ship, but was clearly demonstrating that I had no idea how to utilise the power at my disposal.

Dark Star was right: I didn't know how to use the Sun Heart, and as I fumbled with my ability to shield both myself and Grace as well as to oppose the force trying to sink me into the bay, Dark Star took the opportunity to penetrate my defences. I felt the full power from the whips landing on my body as I left openings in my guard, ripping into me as though I were a lightning conductor in the middle of an electrical storm. I staggered backwards with each blow, but with every step, the black bears and the platform moved closer to where I needed them.

I dropped to my hands and knees, my head falling close to the snow. I raised my eyes and looked at the Sun Heart floating inches from the surface a few feet away as the bombardment of blows broke over my protective shield, bursting into light like fireworks. I wondered if this was really going to work. How could I hope to defeat something that had been created with the sole purpose of destroying anything that stood in its path? I had been trying not to think about what would happen if I failed, but now everything I was doing became horribly clear in my mind: if I could not defeat Dark

Star, this entire world would be destroyed. It would be obliterated as quickly and easily as someone burning a piece of paper.

I rose unsteadily to my feet, letting some of my thoughts escape. I wanted Dark Star to think that I was weak, that I was nearly powerless and close to the end. I was sure that Dark Star would believe this: it was easy to flatter the mind of a creature who had no doubt in their own authority; who believed in the absolute certainty that everything was theirs to command and control and that nothing could oppose them. This was how things had been for millions of years and this was how things would be again.

Dark Star paused in attacking me and I sensed a mind full of triumph. I had been defeated and had therefore forfeited ownership of the Sun Heart. The ferocity of the thoughts bore down on me like the concentrated beam from a lighthouse, burning through me, engulfing me with visions of everything that would take place now that the Sun Heart would no longer be in my possession. Dark Star was gloating in a manner that could only be described as human, showing me what my failure was going to cost. All life would end on our world. It would be as if life had never been, as if the dust and gas swirling around the sun had never formed into a world. There would just be an extra space in the solar system filled with lumps of broken rock.

Dark Star moved off the platform, clearly wanting to finish

me off at close quarters. All other thoughts had gone, leaving nothing but the overwhelming desire to kill me and to take possession of the Sun Heart. The tendrils rose almost dramatically slowly, as if the moment were being savoured.

Although I was weak, although I would have been cut into hundreds of pieces and burnt black by the force of Dark Star's attack if I had a normal body, I was not as weak as I had allowed Dark Star to believe.

And Dark Star was unaware of Amara. I had wrapped her in a cloak of shadows as she rose from the perpetual night of her home at the bottom of the crater, ascending as no more than a swirl of dark water reaching up for the light.

And now, she was here.

Before any of the deadly coils could strike, I hurled Dark Star's mass of cloud and swirling arms back onto the platform with all the force I could muster from the Sun Heart. Dark Star's overconfidence had allowed me the advantage, but I had only moments before Dark Star recovered and broke free.

There was a sudden explosion of snow, ice and water. Two of Amara's colossal tentacles erupted through the surface of the bay on either side of the platform. Her giant, sucker-covered arms wrapped themselves tightly around Dark Star's writhing form and pulled the entire platform, together with the two helpless black bears, down into the waters.

I could feel Dark Star struggling against Amara, trying to rip her apart. But I had moved all of my protective power onto her and there was nothing Dark Star could do. Her grip only became stronger as she dragged her prize lower and lower into the depths. In desperation Dark Star reached out to me. Pure hate and defiance invaded my mind and body like swarms of locusts, devouring everything in their path. I could do little to protect myself without reducing the defences I had placed around Amara. My legs started to buckle and I feared I would not be able to protect Amara for much longer.

But as the Kraken descended further into the crater, Dark Star's power began to suffocate under the growing pressure, and the forces invading me began to ebb away. As Amara approached the lowest depths, the pressure became even more intense and I felt Dark Star leaving my mind completely, slowly diminishing to a single point of essence.

As the last vestiges of life left that ancient body, a great sigh rose up from the depths of the crater, tearing through the waters and bursting from the surface with the sound of countless souls being released from torment. The cries surged up, roaring round and round the bay, faster and faster, until it sounded as if the sky itself was being torn apart.

And then it stopped and there was silence.

I sank to my knees and fell over. I remember being confused by the sight of objects like small black rags falling from the sky, just glimpsed through half-closed eyes, before the exhaustion that was consuming me took me into the blissful peace of unconsciousness.

Chapter 32

Partings

When I opened my eyes again, I found myself looking up at the stars. I felt something on me and turned my head. Grace was standing on my arm and Wind Over Mountain was sitting nearby. I started to say something, but drifted into sleep before I could form any words.

The next time I opened my eyes it was day. Wind Over Mountain hadn't moved. As he came more clearly into focus, I could see dark smears of blood staining the white coat of his head, body and legs. Some of it undoubtedly belonged to others, but I could see a gash running down one of his shoulders that didn't look good.

Grace was also looking battered. There was blood on her chest and some of her flight feathers were missing, but otherwise she seemed to be all right.

The Sun Heart still shone, floating near the ground, two feet from my head. I thought it would have turned itself off when I lost consciousness, but there it was, connected to me and connecting me to everything. I started to reach out to Wind Over Mountain, but remembered that I didn't need to use the Sun Heart to speak to him as I had with the other bears, and felt moreover that he would not appreciate the intrusion.

"I'm sorry," I said, without getting up. "I don't know how

to use the Sun Heart to help either of you."

Wind Over Mountain got slowly to his feet, the pain in his shoulder apparent from the growls that he produced. He limped over to me and looked down with eyes that had lost their usual hostility and contempt.

The Sun Spirit will heal us, he said.

I turned my head to look across the bay towards where I thought everyone else should be. I could make out some vague shapes, one of which I assumed was The Keeper.

"Did anything happen to me while I've been lying here? Did The Keeper come and do something?"

The Sun Spirit came. The Sun Spirit said that your body would heal itself.

Letting Grace hop off to the snow, I pushed myself up into a kneeling position and then gingerly stood up. "And Wind Over Sea and the fox; are they all right?" I asked.

They both fell, he replied.

"Oh," I said, a little shocked by the straightforward simplicity of the words that had formed in my mind. I waited for anything further that Wind Over Mountain might add, but he remained silent. "And The Keeper can save them as well?" I asked.

Wind Over Mountain turned and started walking stiffly off in the direction of The Keeper. *The Sun Heart is needed to do this. You must return it now.*

I stumbled forward and followed Wind Over Mountain

across the snow, the Sun Heart staying its customary two feet in front. Grace was finding it difficult to fly, so I let her rest on my arm. I caught up with Wind Over Mountain and walked by his side. Neither of us spoke. Apart from a few grunts of pain from Wind Over Mountain, the only sound was the wind and the occasionally high-pitched piping call of an Arctic tern flying overhead.

As we got closer I saw The Keeper surrounded by a number of birds and bears. Some were standing, some were lying down. Very few seemed to be undamaged and a small number were clearly lifeless. The snow around them had turned red with their blood, which slowly seeped through the snow to the waters beneath.

I looked up at Wind Over Mountain, but he continued on without any indication that he was touched by the sight.

The two cubs suddenly appeared from somewhere and ran over to us, throwing themselves at Wind Over Mountain's legs. The bear stopped and looked down, then lowered his head and rubbed his nose against each of them before gently pushing them out of the way. The cubs walked behind their father and we all carried on the last few hundred yards to The Keeper.

The Keeper turned towards us. *Does Wind Over Mountain require treatment?*

Wind Over Mountain will wait, came the response and the bear turned and stared at me.

I looked from the bear to The Keeper. "Wind Over

Mountain is waiting for me to return the Sun Heart to you," I said. "He says it is needed to save Wind Over Sea and the fox."

This is true. My ship no longer has enough power to heal them.

I thought about this and something occurred to me. 'Couldn't you have taken the Sun Heart from me while I was asleep?'

No, I could not do this. You had not closed the Sun Heart and I therefore could not take it, The Keeper replied.

"Really?" I said, sceptically. "Dark Star seemed to be of a different opinion."

If you had been killed, Dark Star would have been able to possess the Sun Heart. However, as long as you are alive, only you can close it.

I looked at the Sun Heart and felt comforted by this, as if there was an unbreakable bond between us keeping me safe.

Then the memory of the moments leading up to my father's ship crashing to the ground appeared in my mind. "But what about the captain?" I asked. "It was the captain's hand touching the Sun Heart that made the ship crash."

You witnessed your father's memories?

"Yes, I did."

I have not seen these, The Keeper said. *But what you say does not sound possible. I will know more if you return the Sun Heart to me.*

I paused. "If I return it? You mean that I don't have to

return it?"

I heard Wind Over Mountain growl, but The Keeper spoke over the noise and the bear quietened down.

You are The Keeper now. You do not have to return the Sun Heart. Your father did not want to return it. Before the ship crossed over the field, I sensed that your father thought he could use the Sun Heart to stop wars and prevent suffering in your people. I think you have had similar thoughts.

"Yes, I have. But at the moment I don't even know how to heal Wind Over Mountain or Grace, so I doubt I would be able to do anything worthwhile."

You have learnt much. In time you would learn how to do these things. You would be able to end wars. With the Sun Heart you could stop all the guns in the world from firing, you could feed every person and stop all diseases.

For a moment I imagined all these things; imagined a world where there was no fighting, no hunger, no suffering.

"If I took all the weapons away, people would only fight with spoons and fists. If I fed everyone, I would then become responsible for everything else that is necessary to allow them to live and survive. And in the end I replace a thousand wrongs with one wrong a thousand times worse."

Your father did not see this.

One of those thoughts that kept rising up like a bad taste emerged again. Instead of swallowing it back down I let it come fully to the surface. "Was that why you chose him? Because you knew he wouldn't return the Sun Heart? That he would take it away from here?"

I have no memory of choosing your father and I do not remember wanting the Sun Heart to be taken away from here.

"But it's very convenient, isn't it? My father somehow manages to take the Sun Heart away and hide it, when you knew that someone far more dangerous was going to come along and take it from you."

The same thought also occurred to Dark Star, which was why we fought for so long initially. Dark Star thought I had knowledge of how this had happened.

"And did you?"

Dark Star did not find anything. If Dark Star did not find anything, there was nothing to find.

The Keeper said nothing further. For a while I didn't speak either, letting the seconds add to the weight of the silence. Then I reached up and closed my hand around the Sun Heart, extinguishing the light that had been with me for so long now.

"Here. Take it," I said, holding the Sun Heart out to The Keeper.

Both of The Keeper's arms rose up to take the Sun Heart from me. For a moment it lay in The Keeper's hands; a dull, grey, featureless ball. Then it burst back into light. The Keeper's arms withdrew and the Sun Heart stayed floating in the air.

The Keeper turned back to the animals and a table rose

out of the snow. I watched a goshawk with a broken wing float up and gently land on the table in front of The Keeper.

Instruments of one sort or other appeared and disappeared from the surface of the table like strange flowers living through the seasons in minutes. Torn bones and feathers were drawn together and joined up to create a complete wing. All the instruments withdrew into the table and the goshawk stood up and shook its wings, then sprang into the air towards the southern mountains.

One by one, a wounded bear or bird was lifted through the air and placed in front of The Keeper.

I stood silently, gazing in wonder as each animal was worked on. For the lifeless animals, many more instruments appeared and disappeared from the table, and creatures that had previously been no more than carcasses became whole and started breathing again.

After they had been treated, each animal left the bay, the goshawks flying south and the bears walking off towards the Path of the Ancients.

Each bear turned to me and nodded before leaving. Water Flowing Over Ice stared at me for a long time before inclining her head in farewell, as though wondering how to weave me into the stories that would be written of this day.

Eventually, all of the animals had been treated, including Wind Over Mountain and Grace. The table melted back into the snow and all the blood and debris disappeared, leaving just the unchanging white expanse of snow with myself, Wind Over Mountain, Wind Over Sea, the cubs and the fox standing in a quiet group by The Keeper.

The last to leave was Grace. I watched as she flew off without a glance back towards me. I knew that this was the last time I would see her and that if I travelled through her forest again, she would hide from me as she would from any other person.

My thoughts were interrupted by The Keeper moving closer to me.

I now have all the information from the Sun Heart from the time it left me.

The Keeper paused and I wondered if I was expected to say something, but The Keeper continued.

It will not be comfortable to hear. Would you like some tea?

"No, I would not like some tea!"

As you wish. Just before your father took the Sun Heart, any thoughts or memories I had that related to the plan to stop Dark Star were removed from my mind and stored in the Sun Heart. Dark Star would then be unable to discover these when questioning me or searching my mind. These memories would only exist in the Sun Heart.

A plan? Although I had always imagined this, it was still a shock to hear it. Maybe I should have accepted the offer of tea.

"So there was a plan all the time?"

Yes, there was a plan.

"You controlled my father's actions? And mine?"

This is not true. I controlled some events in your father's life that would restrict or govern some of his choices. I would not have been able to do this once he was in possession of the Sun Heart.

"But my father didn't really take the Sun Heart, did he? You gave it to him and showed him how to use it so that he could carry out your plan."

Yes. I passed control of the Sun Heart to your father and helped him to understand how to use it to escape. These memories were removed from your father before I removed my own memories. Your father was left with only the knowledge of how to use the Sun Heart. I was left with no memory of what I had done and I became as much a part of the plan as your father.

I tried to make sense of this new information.

"You didn't wanted my father to completely escape with the Sun Heart, though? You didn't want him to get home and actually start using it?"

No.

"Because you needed me to come along and find it after Dark Star had arrived."

Yes.

"So the Sun Heart made the captain crash the ship?"

No, this could not have happened. The Sun Heart was instructed to close at that point. What you saw in your father's memories did not take place.

"You changed my father's memories?"

Yes. I reasoned that you would react less favourably if you discovered the ship was crashed deliberately.

"Less favourably?" I opened and closed my mouth a few times, but any attempts at further articulation failed. I realised that I was pacing back and forth in frustration, so I forced myself to stand still and I didn't speak for a few minutes.

"And what about my desire to find my father; was that all made up as well?"

A number of instructions were placed in the Sun Heart to ensure other events were more likely to take place. The dreams given to you by the Sun Heart helped you to locate your father's ship, but I think you always had a desire to find your father. Is this not true?

How could I know what was true anymore?

"So, we were all following the paths laid out for us in a story that you had created to hide the Sun Heart from Dark Star and to use me to defeat him," I said.

We do not know how to create stories. We only work with what is possible and what is not possible. Do you believe there was an alternative way of defeating Dark Star? I have been trying and failing to do this for thousands of years.

I sat down and dug my hands into the substance that was

neither snow nor spaceship, slowly lifting my fingers in and out, watching the grains flowing from my skin like water. I realised that I had as much chance of understanding everything that had happened as I had of understanding how this snow could transform into something capable of travelling between the stars.

"What will you do now?" I asked The Keeper.

I will leave.

"Leave?"

Yes.

I stood up. "Leave the planet?"

Yes.

"Have you collected everything that you need from here?"

No, but your world and thousands of other worlds are safe now. We, The First, are also safe and can continue to our natural end.

"So why are you leaving?"

Although I did not end the life of Dark Star, by allowing you to use the Sun Heart to do this I have broken our laws and must return to answer for this.

"What will happen to you?"

I will lose the Sun Heart.

"This was your sacrifice?"

Indeed. We have both sacrificed much.

I didn't say anything for a while.

"And you say that Dark Star would have destroyed every

world where there was a light in the Galaxy Room of the Citadel."

Yes. No one here on this world, or on all the other worlds, will know of what you did. But my world will know. You will be known as the Radiance of the Worlds; for without you, all of the lights that you saw would no longer shine.

I didn't know what to say. I was thinking of the Sun Heart, of this race of people that could do anything because they had discovered how to unlock the power to mould the building blocks of matter and even life.

I looked up suddenly.

"If you can bring me and the bears and the goshawks back to life, couldn't you do the same for my father and the crew?"

There was a pause and I half expected a cup of tea to materialise from the snow.

This is not possible. Too much damage will have taken place to the mind. If I rebuilt the bodies of these men, there would be no memories for them. They would become like children, with no names, having to learn how to walk again.

I tried to imagine that and had to agree that it didn't sound like a good solution.

"But what about my father? All of his memories are in the Sun Heart. You could rebuild him with his memories."

When you experienced your father's memories, did you think that you were Alfred?

"No, of course not. But I felt what it was like to be Alfred.

He was there."

Alfred wasn't there, though. You were just watching his life. If I put all of Alfred's memories back into his body, it would be the same for him. It would be as if he were someone else watching another life. He wouldn't be Alfred.

"So, you're saying that we are more than just our memories and experiences? What else is there? A soul?"

There is time.

"Time?"

Yes. Although I only exist now, at this moment, I am also only myself in relation to everything that has happened to me in the past. It is the experience of living those moments in time and my relationship to those moments now, which creates the sense of myself.

"This is a lot to take in."

Indeed, but if it were otherwise, I would not still be using this body.

I wasn't sure if The Keeper was trying to be amusing or not, but it seemed unlikely, and I stood there looking up at the mountain, lost in thought.

Eventually I held my arm out, pointing at the pass.

"Can the ship, my father and the remains of the other crew members be brought down from the mountain and buried here, in the dark waters of the bay?"

This can be done, The Keeper replied, turning to face the mountain. For a while nothing happened and I wondered

299

if what I had asked was going to be possible. I looked at the bears and the fox, but they were staring up at the mountain, clearly waiting for something to happen.

I looked back up at the mountain. My eyesight was much keener than it had been, before I was put back together by The Keeper. Even from where we were, I could clearly see the top of the mountain where the ship would cross. But there was nothing to see, just a speck that might have been Grace flying home across the pass.

Then Grace suddenly changed course as if to avoid something. For a moment there was nothing and then, little by little, the battered and rusted stern of *The Daedalus* rose into view and slowly crested the pass. The ship moved leisurely backwards down the mountainside. I saw how sorry-looking and broken it was. Its bows and the bridge were almost completely crushed and the section below the bridge was blackened by the fire I had started. There were bits hanging off the main structure and other parts that had become detached were floating in the air and following in procession behind, like the crazed retinue of an even madder king.

There were some smaller items further behind the ship. I couldn't make them out at first, but I inhaled sharply when I realised they were the bodies of the crew, lifted from their scattered snowy graves and carried along with this vessel that had been their last home.

The procession moved in a stately fashion from the

mountainside to the flat snow covering the bay. It continued
with more speed before coming to a graceful stop not far from
where we were gathered and stayed there, floating a foot or
two above the surface.

*This is everything belonging to the ship and the crew that
was in the mountains,* said The Keeper. *There is no trace of
them left now.*

"Thank you," I said.

I looked at the wreck of the ship and a wave of sadness
washed over me. I wasn't sure if it was related to the state of
the ship or knowing that my father and the other members of
the crew were finally going to be laid to rest and that their
journey had at last reached its end.

They had been caught up in a story over which they had
no control. Like the captain's whiskey glass, they had been
washed around, riding a storm, not knowing where they were
going or how to change direction: unable to see the hand that
was moving them. Except for my father, who believed that he
could replace The Keeper, that he could become the controlling
force. But he was already in a story. By taking the Sun Heart
he had merely moved into a larger glass, being guided by forces
that he couldn't possibly understand.

And me, what story was I in? Could I have made different
choices? Could I have questioned more and accepted less?

The Keeper, who must have known what was going
through my mind, interrupted my train of thought.

Did you wish to say anything before the ship and the crew enter the waters?

I suddenly felt responsible for everything that had happened to these men. Survivor's guilt kicked in. Even though I understood I wasn't responsible, I knew that my father and ten others had been sacrificed all those years ago for me to be standing here this day.

"Can you make it look more like a ship again and lay the men inside?" I asked The Keeper. "I think it's the least they deserve."

The Keeper didn't say anything, but I heard the sound of metal being put under strain and saw the ship straightening in front of my eyes. The bows began to unfold and the bridge rose up from the crushed mass of tangled material it had become. The burnt and rusted metal returned to its original colour and the broken and disconnected parts of the vessel moved into place, joining up with the main structure. Every piece of glass had been gathered up from the mountain and I saw them all swirling around, spinning and shining in the dying light as they reformed the windows of the bridge and the main cabin and the port holes below decks.

Finally, the bodies of the men floated forward and were laid out on the deck. I watched as my father was moved out from the reconstructed bridge, hands still stretched out in front of him, and placed at the very front of the bow.

"Thank you," I said again.

I stared at the ship for what seemed like a very long time. Although part of me ached for the loss of my father and the fate of these men, I realised that I had to accept this as the end of things and that the ship should be allowed to descend silently to the bottom of these waters and rest.

"I seem to have so many memories of these men. I know their story can never be told and I can think of no words that would do them justice."

Very well, The Keeper replied.

The snow and ice beneath the ship parted and she dropped slowly to the surface of the water and continued down into the depths, letting off great gusts of air as she descended.

I turned to speak.

The men will not leave the ship, The Keeper said, anticipating my question. *They will not rise to the surface, nor will Amara touch them or the ship.*

The bubbling surface of the water calmed, then the ice and snow reformed until the bay became flat and smooth once again. The wind picked up and the sun began to fall behind the mountains.

Is there anything else you would ask of me? The Keeper said.

I was sure that he knew what I was going to ask for, but I asked anyway.

*There are many things that you are now capable of doing. I anticipated this request and you will find that you know how *to do this when the time comes.*

This surprised me, but I accepted it as true.

"When will you leave?" I asked.

I will leave now.

"Now?" I said, my voice shaking slightly.

Yes.

I felt something move around my legs and looked around me. The snow had started to flow. From every part of the bay it was converging on a point between where we were standing and the mountains to the north. The pillars of snow that Alfred had thought looked like the pipes of a giant organ started to collapse from the bottom and gently fall into themselves, reminding me of someone carefully demolishing tall chimneys. The combined mass of material added to the pile that was rising up from the surface, turning and growing into a structure that would become The Keeper's spaceship. Every part was changing and reforming to become the outer structure and the inner workings of a craft capable of taking someone through the stars and onto worlds that I had visited only in images.

When every last piece of snow had been put in place, I found myself looking at a pure white ovoid, the size of a cathedral. It was tilted slightly, suspended above the bay in a final act of impossibility.

Like me, the bears and the fox had watched all this in silence. Now it was completed, no one seemed keen to say anything, but I eventually spoke.

"Will you ever return?" I asked.

I will not return. The next Keeper will return one day and I will listen to the sounds of your world from the Galaxy Room.

"So, we just say goodbye?"

Yes, we say goodbye.

The bears and the fox still said nothing, but they bowed and raised their heads slightly as a token of parting.

Goodbye, said The Keeper, turning to them. Then The Keeper turned to face me and said, *Goodbye.*

"Goodbye," I said. It felt strange, knowing that these would be the last words I ever spoke to this being.

The Keeper said nothing further, but turned to the spaceship and moved forwards slowly, then stopped and paused, before coming back to stand in front of me. The Keeper lifted an arm in the same manner as when we first met. The covering over the end of the arm rolled back, revealing the flipper-like hand extended towards me. I was shocked, but I reached out and took hold of The Keeper's hand lightly in my own. The flipper folded around my hand and thumb and we stayed like that for a minute, just holding onto each other, a simple sign of union and trust that spoke louder and more clearly than any words.

"Was anything that you told me true?" I asked, without releasing my grip. "Your reason for being here? What I saw inside the Sun Heart?"

When we cannot know what is true, we are left with belief. What we choose to believe, however, is not as important as why we choose to believe it.

The flipper unfolded and The Keeper's arm was lowered back to the body. This time The Keeper moved immediately and with speed to the spaceship, reaching it within seconds. From where I was I couldn't see how or where The Keeper entered the craft, but after another minute the spaceship disappeared. There was no sound, no flash of lights or shock waves. One moment it was there and the next moment it had gone.

I looked around at the bears and the fox. The fox was suddenly looking very frightened. It backed away from the bears and me and its hackles rose up. The animals had been returned to their true state; they were not under the control of The Keeper and would no longer be able to communicate. Although they weren't taking their eyes from him, the bears weren't moving and were not making any sound. The fox continued to back away slowly, then gave a very fox-like yelp before tearing off in the direction of the mountain pass.

The bears watched as the fox disappeared into the distance, then Wind Over Sea turned slowly and headed off towards the Path of the Ancients with the cubs in tow. Wind Over Mountain stayed where he was, but turned his head and stared at me. I wasn't sure what, if anything, remained of any memory Wind Over Mountain might have of me. I took my chance that something remained and I lowered my head and raised it again, as I had seen the bears and the fox do for The Keeper in parting. Wind Over Mountain didn't move at first, but then, in a moment that will stay with me forever, he lowered his head and raised it, before turning and walking off to join Wind Over Sea.

I remained where I was for a while longer, watching these creatures slowly dissolve into the snow and ice, until that was all there was; just the sea-ice with a small covering of real snow.

Soon the tracks of myself, the fox and the bears would be swept away by the wind and covered over with fresh snow. The bay would became a place with no marks; a place where no one had ever been; a place where nothing had ever happened.

It was a clear night lit by a sky full of stars and a large full moon. I looked up at them and wondered what legends the bears would tell of these times, now that the Night Spirit had been banished back to the deepest depths of the sea and the Sun Spirit had risen up, returning to the Sun once more, until such time as the world was once again threatened by perpetual night.

Chapter 33

The Final Request

"So that's it?" I said breathlessly.

"Yes. That's it."

"And The Keeper will never come back?"

"No."

I was quiet, thinking about everything. It was hard to believe that the entire world was safe because of my uncle. But I had seen much of what he'd told me with my own eyes and, I had to remind myself, he could take his head off.

"What did you ask The Keeper for?" I asked, suddenly remembering.

"Sorry?" Uncle Digit said, puzzled.

"The Keeper asked if you wanted anything, but you didn't say what it was."

Uncle Digit was smiling at me.

"Don't tease me. What did you ask for? And why did The Keeper say that you already knew how to do it?"

He stopped smiling. "I'll show you."

Uncle Digit held up one of his hands and looked at his fingers. "Watch," he said and I saw the top of his index finger begin to glow.

"Now, don't move." He reached down and put his hand behind my back near the bottom of my spine. He closed his eyes and stayed still while I held my breath, not knowing what was happening. After about a minute he removed his hand and opened his eyes. He didn't say anything, but was looking at me intently, as if he expected me to do something.

I was about to ask him what he'd done and what he thought was going to happen when I felt something and sat up straight. I wasn't sure at first what it was, or where it was, but after a few more moments there was a definite tingling sensation in one of my toes. It disappeared and then I felt another in a toe on my other foot.

I looked at my feet and then back up at Uncle Digit.

"What's happening?" I asked in a trembling voice.

Uncle Digit didn't say anything, but his smile broadened as he saw that I was obviously starting to get more tingles down my legs.

I put my hands down and patted my legs.

"Mum!" I shouted. "Mum, come quickly!"

I heard something clatter in the kitchen, then Mum's feet pounding up the stairs.

"What did you do?" I asked Uncle Digit. "I can feel my legs. How did you do it?"

Uncle Digit, still smiling broadly, raised his hands up with both palms facing out, like a conjurer showing that they weren't hiding anything.

"It's magic!"

Epilogue

The man turned the wheels of his chair backwards and moved away from the computer. He looked at his hands, hands that were now decades older than those of the child he'd just left on the screen.

He gripped the wheels of his chair again, slightly tighter than he normally would have. This was an important day and he needed to remind himself how far he'd come.

He gave a small laugh as he wheeled himself forward, remembering how everything had started after his uncle had come back from a photo assignment near the Arctic Circle. His uncle had been full of tales of the mountains and the cold, but had also come back missing one part of a finger.

Then, after returning to the Arctic for another stint, his uncle came back with part of a different finger missing. He was shocked that his uncle seemed so unconcerned by this.

"Dear Boy," he'd said, "as long as I can still take photos I don't mind what I lose."

"Yes, but wouldn't it be funny if you came back saying 'you'll never guess what happened to me this time, Dear Boy' and you took your head off?"

He remembered that they had laughed about this for quite a while. But then they started imagining ways in which this might have happened and why.

And that was it: from then on, all of their talk was about

how his uncle could have lost his head and got it put back on again.

They had spent days working out different story-lines and possibilities. All the ideas went into small notebooks that provided ideas, not just for Uncle Digit, but for a whole host of other stories. Stories that had started out as simple conversations full of light and laughter, but that had been the pure springs from which his imagination had flowed, becoming the streams and rivers of tales and stories: the magic of words, creating and sparking ideas and imaginations, not just in himself, but in the minds of others caught up in the shimmer of stardust brushed into the mind's eye.

And it was his uncle who had prompted him to remember what the little girl had said at the healing waters and the way this echoed the fairy tale his grandmother used to tell.

After that, he learned to keep the magic inside the stories. And now, after all these years, it was coming full circle.

He left the house and manoeuvred himself into his car. He put the car into full auto–drive mode and sat back, tapping the steering wheel absentmindedly in time to the music that was playing to calm himself.

But this wasn't easy; he'd been waiting for this day all his life.

The day when technology caught up with the touch of Uncle Digit's hands and became the magic that gave him a chance to walk again.

The day when, as he felt the first pulses of feeling travel down his legs, he would look in speechless astonishment at the smiling surgeon, holding out his hands like a conjurer showing there was nothing up his sleeves.

"Look," he'd say. "No magic!"

Acknowledgements

The book that you have hopefully just read and enjoyed is a very different book from the one I first finished, a mere nine drafts ago! The differences are such that it's hard to imagine I could have ever thought the book was "finished" at any previous stage.

For help getting me here, I am eternally grateful to Fiona Lloyd, Ellie Steer, Rufus Purdy and Emer Workman, all of whom provided invaluable feedback and recommendations that helped me to create completely new drafts of the book.

A huge thank you to my editor, Nick Hodgson, who pushed me to make bolder changes and who rounded all the rough edges and gave the book a shape and style I know I couldn't have come close to on my own.

Whoever said "don't judge a book by the cover" probably wasn't thinking of the occasions were the cover was actually better than the writing it illustrated and I have to thank Zsuzsa for providing cover art and illustrations that surpassed anything I imagined.

Thanks to Kate Ellis for not laughing at my attempts at writing in a Yorkshire accent and for providing an accurate version for Dan Sykes, the cook of *The Daedalus*.

Thanks also to Doug Knox for giving me the two pieces of advice that will always stay with me and which I hold in my mind every time I put words on the screen.

My family deserve special mention and should be given medals for putting up with my constant Uncle Digit readings and conversation hijacks. Thanks for giving me a boost when I needed it.

And thank you for buying, or even looking at, this book. Please pass it on.

About the Author

Jeremy Hullah grew up in the rural Midlands, where he spent a lot of time dreaming about being a pianist or a writer, or something equally unattainable without the required level of effort. After proving beyond all doubt that education was not something that came naturally, he moved to London where he worked on building sites for a few years before retraining in IT. Now, many years later, he works for a bank in the City, writing books on the train to and from his home in East Sussex, where he spends whatever time is left cycling around the countryside, dreaming up ideas for new books to keep his two boys entertained.

Follow the author on Instagram

@JEREMYHULLAH

Or visit digitpublications.com

Coming later in 2024

The second book in the Uncle Digit series of
adventures

Uncle D^{i}git
and the
Song of the Desert

The sands had been advancing for many years now. Most
of the city lay submerged beneath dunes that stretched as
far as the eye could see and that had already engulfed the
great cities of Apa'Mau and Apa'Ko.

Only the topmost twenty feet of the immense
Temple of the Sun, tallest of all the buildings in Apa'Tui
could be seen, the golden capstone of the pyramid
reflecting the sun that burned down incessantly.

Where once the light from the stone had shone
brightly amidst the buildings and gardens of a proud city,
declaring to the world that here was the centre of all
things, it now flashed like a warning beacon as the city
slowly drowned under the sea of sand.

Inside the highest room of the temple, just below
the capstone, a man sat on a throne. A girl sat on the steps

near him. The sands that had already climbed most of the steps leading up to the throne started to tickle her feet.

The man turned to the girl. "Are you comfortable, my daughter?" he asked.

The girl looked at her father, the great king Cho'Te'Nefa, his broad nose powerful and righteous, his brown skin still clear and not yet aged to soft leather. The king looked down at her with tenderness. There was nothing about him that showed the slightest fear or concern for the fate that drew ever closer to them.

"I am comfortable, father," she replied.

The girl looked above the king's eyes, to the headdress that sat on his long dark hair: ostrich feathers for a mind, quick and direct; papyrus for ideas, versatile and useful; everything threaded through and bound with fresh water pearls for dreams and bright sequins for laughter.

She wondered why these qualities had not been enough to save them.

"Will it be long now, father?" she asked.

The king looked at the sand flowing in through the last of the openings in the sides of the temple. He looked directly above his head to the small circle of blue sky that could be seen through the hole in the capstone and felt the tiny impact as a few grains of sand that had managed to find their way in from the very top of the pyramid fell onto his cheeks.

"It will not be long now, my child," he said.

At night they heard the howling, as the wind drove fresh waves of sand against the walls of the temple, and they heard the constant trickle as the sand streamed down the walls, like the rustling of leaves in a gentle breeze or the sound of people dancing in silken robes.

In the morning the sand was at the foot of the throne and the girl got up, brushed the sand from her legs and sat next to her father on the great chair.

"Raxa has forgotten Bibika," the girl said, holding up a small doll dressed in a bright red robe with coloured stones stuck in her hair, which she had taken from beneath her own robe. "I found it under the Chest of Souls the other day."

She knew she wasn't supposed to go near the Chest of Souls, but felt that the Spirits would not mind in the circumstances.

Her father stroked her hair and said nothing about her misdeed. "Keep it safe for her," he said softly. "Your sister will return one day and she will want to know that Bibika has been looked after."

Would Raxa return? the girl wondered. *And why had she been commanded to leave?*